Matthew & Christina

a love story

R. Ann Steel

ISBN 978-0-9737628-9-1

Editing and layout by Lee Thompson Editing+.

Cover photos courtesy of
Melanie Mauer (front)
Boris Smokrovic (back)

Butterfly Books
Saint John, New Brunswick
Canada

To contact the author:
ann@butterflybooks.media

Prologue

The windshield exploded, showering glass over the passengers. They screamed as the Pathfinder careened across the road shrouded in a cloud of dust and coming to a sudden stop as it rammed into the bank. Vivienne was propelled forward. The engine died. When Vivienne regained her seat, she saw that the driver was not moving. She watched in horror as the front of his shirt became increasingly red. She realized he was dead. The two other women in the back of the vehicle started to climb out through the only working door. Vivienne fell out of the front passenger door to her knees and was helped up by one of the other women.

They squinted into the rapidly sinking sun, scanning the horizon to see where the shot had come from, spotting three figures carrying weapons silhouetted against the horizon. "Holy hell," Mary yelled at them. "Are we are being kidnapped?"

Vivienne ran to the back of the vehicle and wrestled the lift gate open looking for something, anything that could be used as a weapon. She resigned herself to the tire iron that lay there.

As they approached, their eyes were the only thing visible beneath their turbans. Vivienne was sure one was leering at her. The three women stood, not knowing what to expect, when a pick-up truck appeared from the same direction as the turbaned men. For a brief moment Vivienne thought the pick-up had come to rescue them but that was not the case. The truck slid to a halt, sending a cloud of dust high into the air as one of the men shouted at the driver in Arabic.

They approached the girls, waving their guns and laughing. Vivienne stood her ground, tightening her grip on the tire iron. She looked at the one she thought was the leader and said in English, "We are aid workers on our way to the compound to deliver food to the refugees there."

He shook his head and indicated with the butt of his gun

to his ear that he did not have a clue what she was saying. Tears sprang to her eyes as she looked at the other two women beside her. The kidnappers grabbed them by their arms, proceeded to tie the wrists of the two women together. They struggled but the kidnappers' grip was fierce. They were herded toward the back of the pick-up, but refused to climb in as the leader spoke rapidly. Vivienne's friends were lifted bodily into the bed of the truck.

When one got within striking distance she swung the tire iron and hit him on the shin as hard as she could. She knew it wouldn't make a bit of difference but she was not going down without a fight. He screamed in pain and in the process of grabbing the tire iron pulled her arm so hard that it ripped the sleeve off her shirt. He then slammed the butt of the rifle on the side of her head, knocking her unconscious.

Chapter 1

The downtown office on the twentieth floor was dark, the only light coming from Matthew Bryson's desk lamp. His staff had all gone home, as it was now past eight o'clock. Flickering shadows played across his young, handsome face, illuminating a sad expression. He had been watching the montage of pictures on his laptop for the past ten minutes, unable to turn away.

Earlier, he had placed Vivienne's favorite flowers, Gerbera daisies, on her grave and sat there unable to hold back the tears.

In the year since her death, Matthew had been trying to make sense of his life without her.

The company that he owned, Midnight Security, had become *the* premier security company. It had a reputation around the world for always getting the job done. He had built that reputation carefully, never failing to deliver the promised result, which had ranged from gaining the freedom of hostages to making sure that dignitaries visiting foreign countries were well protected.

He was an exceptional CEO, mindful of what was needed to achieve the reputation his company had. Which was why, when it all went wrong in the most important mission of his life, Matthew had not been able to forgive himself. He had failed monumentally and it weighed heavily on him. He had lost the drive, the ambition that had sustained him in the past. It all seemed pointless now. He closed his laptop, took a deep breath to clear his head, deciding that he had to stop this self-inflicted torture and go home. He straightened his tie, buttoned his suit's jacket, put on his overcoat and left the darkened office.

By the time he reached the parking garage he felt somewhat better. Climbing into his SUV he stopped for a moment to collect his thoughts and decided he'd rather go to his favorite bar than home. Since Vivienne's death he had been in no hurry to get home after work. Pulling his collar up and putting his head down against the rain, he arrived at the small bar that was close to his building and was greeted by Harry. He came here more than was healthy, but he liked the fact that Harry knew his name and placed his favorite drink before him as soon as he was settled at the bar. Single malt scotch always hit the spot.

It was quite busy for a Wednesday evening. All of the bar stools were taken except for the one next to him and another at the far end.

The scotch started to have an effect and he was beginning to mellow when he sensed a movement next to him. He hadn't taken much notice of what was going on around him but a soft, feminine voice asked if the seat was taken he turned and stared into the most amazing pair of large, dark, almond-shaped eyes he had ever seen. His heart missed a beat, just one, but it was enough to take him by surprise and he felt a little disconcerted, thinking that maybe it was the scotch that had done that.

She placed her phone on the bar and waited for Harry. "Merlot please," she said when Harry arrived.

She turned to Matthew and said, "Cheers, hope you had a good day."

"Not really, but cheers anyway. Hope yours was good."

There it was again! Another missed heartbeat.

"It was, actually. By the way, my name is Christina. This is a very cozy bar. I've never been here before."

Thinking he would have remembered if she had, he replied, "I like it here. I'm Matthew, I come here quite often. I live just a block away."

What the hell am I doing giving away that kind of information?

She did not say anything more, but sat sipping her wine. She appeared to be deep in thought when her Blackberry buzzed. She answered. "I was wondering if I was going to hear from you; yes I'm at the bar. I'll come over right away."

She gathered her purse and Blackberry and slid off the seat. "Nice to meet you, Matthew."

"Same here. Be careful out there."

She turned and smiled. "Thanks, I always am."

Matthew watched her make her way to the door. When he turned back, he noticed his reflection in the mirror behind the bar.

Is that really me? You look like hell, Bryson!

Matthew stayed for one more drink. He parked, rode the elevator up to his penthouse suite, images of dark eyes floating through his mind, making him feel uncomfortable. Why was that?

The elevator came to a sudden halt and brought him back to the present. He steeled himself to walk into his empty apartment.

Once inside he put his keys on the rack then moved down the hallway to his bedroom.

All that was left of her in this room was the portrait photo he had on his dresser. He touched it gently and smiled.

There you are. Miss you, love you, always.

A long hot shower helped ease the constant pain in his left thigh, but did nothing for the one in his heart.

Heading for the couch wearing only black silk pyjama bottoms, he switched on the TV. He checked his iPhone for messages. There were none, not surprising as he only had one field operation at this time. At least he could relax somewhat. Things had been hectic of late. He and Dan had been reviewing their training courses and had been revising some. They would have to go to the training facility soon, in order to implement the new courses.

He hated being here alone. He didn't want to remember but he didn't want to forget.

He began to think about the girl who sat beside him at the bar. He closed his eyes and realized she had not given a last name. He could not forget her eyes and asked himself if he was being unfaithful to Vivienne.

Chapter 2

Christina left the bar and hurried to her meeting. She always made sure her articles were as accurate as humanly possible and needed this information.

Her informant had given her directions. She programmed it into her GPS and arrived at the rendezvous in record time.

He waited under the exit ramp, nervous as he stood behind the pillar. Keeping alert, he took time to reflect on his decision to reveal information to this particular journalist. He had been under cover for over two years and had developed a trust with his so-called boss, Bruno. He had seen the level of human trafficking escalate in the past year and it was time for some heat to be directed toward Bruno's outfit. His boss at the police department, Detective AJ Albert, was all for exposing this organization.

He had never met the journalist before but she had covered a murder that he'd been investigating, and after reading her article in *In the Know*, he heard through the grapevine that she was looking for information.

The sound of footsteps approaching interrupted his train of thought.

When she got to the location and couldn't see anyone she started to feel uneasy. She parked some distance from the ramp and, before exiting her car, took her gun from the glove compartment and placed it behind her back, in her waistband. She felt more apprehensive than usual and the feel of the hard cool metal gave her comfort. She had done this sort of thing many times during her career as a journalist, but never in such a clandestine manner. A member of the local gun club and a brown belt in Grav Maga, she had never really been frightened before, although there were times when she should have been.

It was eerily quiet under the off ramp, and darkness surrounded her. All Christina could hear as she walked towards the support column was the sound of her footsteps and cars passing overhead. Their headlights pierced the blackness.

Peering, listening closely, she moved ahead cautiously. Stepping around one of the columns she almost let out a scream as she saw, illuminated in a pool of light, his lifeless face.

Christina pulled her gun but no one was there. She turned and ran back to her car, her heart thundering in her chest and desperately trying to catch her breath as she fumbled with the lock.

She was shaking and hyperventilating as she slid in behind the wheel, closed and locked her door and sat there for what seemed like forever. "Oh God what do I do now?" She knew he had taken an enormous risk coming to meet her, but he had assured her he had taken every precaution necessary and that their meeting would not be discovered.

Taking a deep breath and trying to steady her hand, she put the key in the ignition. Her mind reeling, she reached the highway, reasoning that if they wanted her dead they would have stayed there and done the job. Did they know where she lived?

She knew how to use her gun and to even take down an attacker using her martial arts skills but this was new territory. Her adrenalin was pumping and she was speeding, but traffic was light. She checked her rear view mirror, saw several cars following her. How would she know if one of them was after her? Breathing deeply, she concentrated on what was in front and not what was behind.

Half an hour later, she arrived in the quiet neighbourhood on the south side where she lived in a small apartment block of only six units. She knew everyone there and as she approached her street she slowed and scanned all the vehicles, looking for any that may be out of place. God, she was such an amateur when it came to doing this stuff. How was she going to keep herself safe?

She parked close to the entrance, glad that the lot was well lit. She removed her gun and set it in her purse. She punched in the access code and was glad when she was finally inside. She felt much better as she took the elevator to the second floor and when she arrived at her apartment she breathed another sigh of relief. She made sure that the deadbolt was on. In fact, she checked it twice.

Taking off her coat and kicking off her shoes, Christina went into the kitchen and poured herself a glass of wine, gulping down a mouthful as she seated herself on her couch. It was close to midnight and she had been going since seven this morning. She checked the news but didn't see anything that alarmed her.

Turning down the volume, she sat back.

She began to shiver. She tried to calm herself by deliberately directing her thoughts to the bar, a much less threatening encounter, the one that involved emerald eyes and a sexy voice. Finishing her wine, suddenly overcome with tiredness, she decided to head to bed, placing her gun on her bedside table. She fell into a troubled sleep, images of her dead informant flashing across her mind.

Chapter 3

Matthew woke early. As was his habit he dressed in his track pants t-shirt and running shoes, put on his wind-breaker, gathered his iPod and headed out for a brisk run, selecting his favorite music as he rode the elevator to the main entrance. Looking outside he saw that the sky had cleared overnight and it was a fine dry day now, great for running. Taking off towards the park some three miles away he set up a steady pace and before long found his rhythm. Running had been part of his life since his days in the armed forces. It helped to organize his thoughts and prepare him for what lay ahead in his work day. Having reached the park in what seemed like no time at all, he decided to run around the lake before heading back home. He was glad that yesterday was behind him.

He had received a text from his sister early this morning asking how his day had been and letting him know that Sara was missing him. He had not seen his niece for over two weeks. He apologized, wrote that he would try to do better.

Back at his apartment, he turned on the coffee machine and while it brewed he headed to the shower, feeling that old familiar pain in his left leg. It never went away completely and was exacerbated by his running. Nevertheless, he continued to run fearing that if he didn't he would end up with a worse pain. It was just one of those irritating things he had to deal with. While shaving, he mentally began to organize his agenda for the day.

He selected a blue shirt and navy suit easily but had trouble deciding which tie to wear. He went with a silk tie, with navy and red stripes. Matthew had always asked Vivienne's opinion on his tie selection and she would laugh and say, "What would you do without me?"

Now he knew.

Preparing his breakfast, he half listened to the news. He looked up when he heard the announcer describe the murder scene. A body had been discovered under exit ramp 233, the victim shot between the eyes. There weren't a lot of murders in the city, so it was big news.

At his office his secretary Anne looked up as he greeted her with his usual disarming smile. "Good morning, Mr. Bryson," Anne said. She held a special affection for her boss and knew that he was still grieving over the death of his wife. Nonetheless, she lived in hope. He didn't notice the way she seemed to blush slightly and how her eyes shone a little too brightly when he spoke. to her. For now, she was content to be the most efficient secretary he ever had. Once he was settled in his office, Anne brought in his mail and reminded him of his afternoon appointment with the president of First City Bank, to discuss the security there. He opened his laptop and fired it up. He saw his screen saver load and smiled at the picture of Vivienne that smiled back at him. Yesterday he had decided enough was enough, and he would really try hard to move on with his life; so, to that end, he put her out of his mind and set about answering his email.

An hour later he was done and looked out of his office door for Dan, his closest adviser. Dan and Matthew had served together in the Special Forces and had survived some dangerous situations. They had trusted each other with their lives

Matthew loved Dan Gates with all his heart and he had been so happy for him when he had married Jane. Already married to Vivienne, he could only hope that Dan would be as happy as he was. After much soul searching, Dan chose retirement over re-signing with the Special Forces for another three years. Jane was unhappy with the lifestyle they had, never knowing what he was up to or where he was half the time. For Matthew, Dan's decision meant he would not have his most trusted friend by his side anymore. He continued in the Special Forces until the end of his contract some nine months later and then followed Dan's lead. Vivienne was naturally happy at his decision.

Matthew started Midnight Security that same year and asked Dan to join him. They had missed the excitement. They hired the best, paying them well and in return had been rewarded with complete loyalty and dedication.

Their reputation for getting the job done grew, and Matthew and Dan began to command larger fees. They both enjoyed the fruits of their labour: Dan lived in an exclusive gated community in a large comfortable house with Jane and two kids; Matthew had, up until his Vivienne's death, been deliriously happy in one of the most sought-after penthouse suites in the city. He had been able to give Vivienne everything she wanted and his last gift to her had been her new car, a Lexus in her favorite colour, red.

He went out to ask Anne if Dan had arrived yet. "Not yet, Mr. Bryson. He's attending a parent-teacher meeting this morning, but he'll be in in about half an hour. Shall I tell him you want to see him?"

"Yes please. Thanks. I'll be in my office." She smiled at him and went back to her current project.

Forty-five minutes later Dan sat on the couch in Matthew's office.

"Morning, Matt, you wanted to see me?"

"Yes. How was the parent-teacher meeting?"

"I never understand what they are for. You only get five minutes per teacher and they never say much. I guess Amelia must be doing alright, otherwise we would have been there longer."

Matthew wondered what parenthood would be like, then continued.

"Yesterday I met with Conrad Hyatt, the president of Impala Oil, and he wants us to review his security measures at his facility in Sudan. Who do you think would be the best person to send? Conrad wants us do this PDQ as he feels the rebels are on the move. It's a very unstable place right now."

"Well, Ty is in Egypt. I guess he's the closest. Also the most qualified to review oil facilities."

"Can I leave it up to you? Let me know what he thinks."

Dan left, and Matthew, seated in his office chair overlooking the city, remembered the many occasions when he and Dan had gone on a mission without much notice. Perhaps they should be going on this one? He rubbed his aching thigh and returned to his computer. He went online and began to familiarize himself with the Sudan. He was apprehensive after finding out how unstable the country was. He knew it was more or less a failed state, but had been unaware of just how unstable it must really be.

After digesting the information, the rest of his day went by uneventfully and he left the office around six.

His phone rang just as he was fastening his seatbelt. Looking at the call display, he answered, "Hi, Mum."

"Hello, darling, how are you today? I know yesterday must have been hard for you so I didn't call, as I was sure you preferred to keep to yourself. You never were one to share. Well, not until you met Viv anyway."

"I made it through, Mum. Bad day but I'm trying to do better from now on. The only thing is Thanksgiving is coming up..."

"You are going to come this year, aren't you? I hate to think of you on your own."

Matthew breathed in a long breath and took his time before answering.

"I'll think about it, Mum. I'm not sure at the moment. You know what I was like last year. I'll let you know by Saturday."

A silence ensued; he could not think of anything else to say, so all he said was, "Say hi to Dad for me. Bye for now. Love you, Mum."

It occurred to him she was the only person he said that to these days.

He programmed in some of his favorite rock music, Queen, cranked the volume and drove directly home, keeping to his resolution to try to change the habits that were impeding his recovery

As he rode the elevator for some reason he remembered that girl again.

He entered his penthouse, put his keys on the rack and, being a creature of habit, headed to the bedroom to change out of his suit. This time he looked at Vivienne's picture and resisted the temptation to touch it. He still could not refrain from saying, "Miss you. Love you always." Baby steps, he thought. He dressed in jeans and a T-shirt, poured himself a Glen Fiddich, and went to the kitchen. Turning on the kitchen TV he set about cooking, making a mental note to keep his ear open for the word Sudan or murder victim.

Sudan never did come up but murder victim did. He listened as the reporter and the police spokesman related the latest developments. No real answers yet but a couple of leads were being pursued. No details were being released at this time.

He was just starting to clear away the dishes when his iPhone rang.

"Hi, Matt, thought I would update you on Ty and Sudan. He says he'll take his team there on Saturday. He thinks it'll still be safe then but can't guarantee anything. He hopes he won't need any more resources but put us on notice that that might be the case. So, we need to put some more guys on standby. Hope that's OK with you?"

"Sure, we'll meet in the morning. Have a great evening. Say hi to Jane for me. See you at the office."

He was about to say goodbye when Dan said, "Where are you by the way?"

"Home. I thought I would try it and see how I make out."

"That's a change. How's it going?"

"Not too well, but I made a promise to myself and I'm going to give it a try."

Matthew ended the call on a sigh and immersed himself in the task preparing a list of suitable people to put on standby. He looked at the clock on his laptop; it was only nine-thirty. He had always liked being in his penthouse suite but now he found it too big and cold, something like his bed.

He Googled Sudan. There was a host of information available. None of it was encouraging.

He knew that the names on his list were up to the task but as he prepared for bed he wondered about the wisdom of his decision.

CHAPTER 4

"Judy, how about dinner at Leo's? Good. See you there."

On her way home she had decided to call her best friend, thinking it would be a pleasant distraction.

What *was* it her informant was going to tell her?

Christina wasn't easily frightened. She rationalized that if anything was going to happen, it probably would have by now.

Judy was already seated facing the window, waving at her a she passed by.

They ordered a bottle of Merlot.

They were immersed in conversation when Christina looked up just as a tall handsome man dressed in a grey suit with a red tie came in and was escorted by the hostess to his table next to the wall. Her eyes followed him as she carried on her conversation with Judy.

After finishing dinner, Judy excused herself and headed to the washroom. Christina's gaze was drawn to him. She noticed his amazing emerald eyes. She caught her breath just for a second. Realization dawned on her. She had sat next to him in that small bar just two nights ago. He didn't look as sad tonight and he certainly made her heart race a little just as he had then.

"Hello!! Where were you?"

Smiling at Judy she said, "Oh, I was just checking out the eye candy. He has the most amazing green eyes, doesn't he?"

Judy turned and, taking a quick glance at him, replied, "Yes. Why? Do you know him?"

"No not really. I sat next to him in a bar two nights ago when I was running down a lead for an article I'm doing."

"And...?"

"We exchanged first names. He seemed rather sad. Odd, him being here tonight."

Matthew had chosen to eat at Leo's because it was close to his office and anyway, he really liked the steak. His pact with himself was wavering slightly but he justified eating out as it was Friday night.

He looked over and was surprised that he recognized her. Suppressing a small smile, he shifted in his seat.

Matthew was ready to leave before they were. He asked for his check and rose from his seat. He left a generous tip on the table and, putting on his overcoat as he walked past, he said, "I hope your meeting went well the other night."

Judy watched him walk to his SUV. Observing his strong frame and the way he carried himself, she concluded military.

"He could put his shoes under my bed any day. Wonder if he's married?"

"Yes he could. And I don't know if he's married. He should be, because who could pass that up? Handsome, isn't he."

Back in her apartment, feeling more like her old self again, she sat on the couch and closed her eyes for just a minute. Her head filled with images of him.

When Matthew got home, he settled in his living room with a nightcap, remembered his mother needed an answer. He had originally decided he would decline this year. Last year he was in no shape to go anywhere. He had just buried Vivienne and he could not even function that whole week. Today he thought he would make his mother happy and go.

Picking up his phone, he scrolled down his contacts and hit speed dial. No answer. He left a message and promptly regretted saying yes. How was he going to handle this? Was he strong enough? He had done a dismal job Wednesday. However, Thanksgiving was more than a week away. He still had time to change his mind.

Having agreed to speak to the members of the local journalist organization regarding personal safety when travelling in foreign countries, he spent the weekend working on his presentation. Organizing his agenda took some time but Matthew didn't mind, he had no love for weekends anymore.

Running on Monday morning, he was aware of the sharpness that was in the air. Returning to his apartment he put on the coffee pot and took a shower.

The ever present question popped into his head. What to wear? He was tempted to go the casual route because journalists, as far as he knew, didn't seem to wear suits and ties or power suits or dresses. So he went with a casual black sport shirt and blue jeans, grey sport jacket, and black slip-on shoes and hoped he looked acceptable. He usually ran this sort of thing by Vivienne.

Before he got to his desk Dan appeared at his side, falling in step with him as they walked toward his office.

"Morning Matt, I heard from Ty last night. He called. It's not good. He wants us to send reinforcements.

"The whole situation is very volatile and the rebels are getting closer to the oil field. The locals are not that highly trained and Ty would prefer our own men. At least he knows what they are capable of. I called Jaguar Air charter and Ken is willing to fly them in. We need to talk to Conrad Hyatt, to let him know this is going to cost him and make sure we have his OK."

Matthew moved to his desk, passing Anne on the way. No greeting, as this morning he was in operation mode. The adrenaline pumped as his mind slipped into top gear. "OK Dan. Let me contact Conrad now and I will get back to you in a few."

He sat down, fired up his laptop, dumped his files on his desk, removed his coat, took out his phone, found Hyatt's number in his contacts list.

Conrad answered immediately.

"Matt, I was just about to call you. I heard from my man in charge. Thanks for getting your men there as fast as you did."

"We were lucky Ty was in Egypt. Made the journey less complicated. He contacted us last night and requested more resources, mostly manpower. I'm calling to let you know that we can get more men on the ground but it will cost you."

There was a silence for a minute on the other end and then Conrad said, "OK, I'll have to live with it if I'm going to have any peace of mind. Have to keep my employees safe."

"That's why you hired the best, Conrad. I will let Dan know he can go ahead with our plan. I will e-mail you details as they become available. Dan is a master at this organizational stuff."

Matthew leaned back in his chair, which let out its usual small squeak. He looked out into the office. It was alive and buzzing today. Everyone doing what they did best, getting this operation off the ground. He felt a surge of pride knowing that he and Dan were responsible.

He buzzed Dan, who arrived looking flushed. "I've spoken to Conrad, Dan, and he's fine with it so you can go ahead and firm up plans with Jaguar."

"Great, I'll give the go ahead to contact everyone on the list. I'll let you know the ETA as soon as I can." With that he left the office hurriedly, already dialing his cell phone.

Now that there was a lull in the flurry of activity, Matthew took a deep breath and turned to his laptop, noting Vivienne's picture. He remembered how she always reacted when he told her he was off somewhere. He remembered the immediate look of concern on her face, how she would get very quiet. Invariably, there was no time to prepare for his leaving, as the very nature of what he did meant urgency was a priority. When he was ready to leave the house she always kissed him passionately and told him she loved him and that he better come back in one piece.

No matter when he got the call, or where he was, he would make sure he saw her before leaving. Sometimes that was hard to do but he always managed it, even if it meant employing Skype. He thought of the wives or girlfriends of his men doing that very same thing right now. Not dwelling on that for too long, he opened up his emails and began working on them. Routine stuff really, as most of the ones relating to the current operation would be handled by Dan.

Before he knew it, it was lunch time. Anne came in to remind him of his lecture at two in conference room one at the convention center. He thanked her, dug out his file containing his notes and moved to the couch in his office where he began reviewing it making sure that his presentation was in order. He packed up his laptop and set it on the couch then buzzed Dan again and when he arrived asked him for a progress report. Dan relayed that everything was going well, no major snags yet, emphasizing the "yet." Invariably, there would be obstacles to overcome on any mission they embarked on. Matthew thanked him and informed him of his whereabouts this afternoon.

"Good luck on the lecture. I hope they take note of your information – journalists have a dangerous job these days. They're a special breed. I'll text you with developments."

Matthew grabbed his laptop and his coat. He stopped for some take out, eating on his way to the convention center, then parked underground, finishing his burger and coke before gathering up his laptop. He took the elevator to the third level and followed the signs and was greeted by a distinguished-looking man, about his height, whose name tag read, "Hi my name is Malcolm Yates" followed by "International Journalist Federation." Matthew noted with some relief that Malcolm was also dressed in jeans.

He approached Matthew and extended his right hand. "Welcome, you must be our speaker, Matthew Bryson."

Matthew nodded and they shook hands.

"You're here in plenty of time. Hate to keep them waiting. Busy people, journalists, you know."

Matthew was used to being early for appointments. Old habits die hard.

Malcolm ushered Matthew towards the dais. A large screen hung on the wall at the back of the dais.

"Hope this is OK. Do you need the screen?"

"Yes, I have a Power Point here, so I'll just queue that up and I'll be ready."

While he was absorbed in setting up, his audience had started to arrive, entering quietly. Matthew continued to review his notes, head down, illuminated by the bright overhead light.

Lifting his head, he began to survey the audience. His heart did that stutter again. He kept his gaze on her as he began. "Good afternoon, my name is Matthew Bryson and I own Midnight Security. As you have probably deduced, we are in the business of providing personal security, and we are very good at it.

"I have been asked to impart useful practical information that will help to keep you safe when you are on assignment, particularly overseas."

He concentrated on his Power Point and notes as much as he could and fifty minutes later he was taking questions. When he finished with the questions and started packing up, he felt someone beside him.

Catching a whiff of jasmine, he looked up, held her gaze for a moment and said, "So you're a journalist are you?" Shuffling awkwardly, trying to regain his composure, he smiled and asked, "Do you have a question for me?"

"No," she smiled engagingly back at him. "But, since we've run into each other three times in five days I think it's time for a formal introduction. My name is Christina Melville. I'm a freelance writer and I found your presentation quite informative."

"Well, you know my name already, but by way of formal introduction...", he paused, held out his right hand, smiling his widest smile, "Matthew Bryson. I'm very pleased to meet you."

She hesitated before taking his outstretched hand with a firm grip that surprised Matthew. Her hand was warm and her touch made him tingle.

"Nice to meet you, Matthew. Who knows, we may see each other again the way things are going."

"You never know."

Sliding behind the wheel of his SUV, he ran his fingers through his hair.

He arrived back at the office just as some of the staff were on their way home. He had kept an eye on his phone, which he had placed on the lectern during his presentation, and was satisfied everything was in Dan's capable hands.

Seated at his desk, he let out a long silent whistle and composed himself before he buzzed Dan's office. Dan appeared a few minutes later with an update.

"Well, the plane took off about half an hour ago. So they are expected in Sudan sometime the day after tomorrow. Ty checked in as well and reported he was making progress with some of the upgrades to security around the drill site. He's identified the major flaws and when our guys arrive he'll feel a lot better."

"Thanks, Dan."

On the way out, Dan said over his shoulder, "How was the lecture?"

"Oh it went very well." He restrained a small smile. "Those journalists are something else. Interesting bunch."

Matthew did some housekeeping with his emails and then sent one to Conrad Hyatt, detailing the mission so far. He texted Ty to let him know that he was pleased with what he had heard and that he hoped things wouldn't escalate before the rest of them arrived. "Think we can go home now," said Dan. "Communications seem to be better than expected." That left one less thing for them to have to deal with.

Matthew was edgy when an operation was in progress. He felt helpless, not being there. He knew how wrong things could go.

Once away from the office he was able to get some time to process what had happened at the lecture. He was still surprised at his physical reaction to Christina. After all, it was only days since he had felt the lowest he had ever felt. He asked himself if his resolution had anything to do with his unexpected reaction. Perhaps he had begun to allow himself to let some light in.

He ate out again at Leo's. Her face swam through his mind's eye unexpectedly as he placed his order.

Driving home, guilt was getting the better of him again. Was he dishonouring Vivienne's memory? He would always love her and that was a fact of his life.

As the week progressed, the memory of the incident with Christina took a back seat to the ongoing operation in the Sudan. Things were going as well as could be expected and the other members of Midnight had arrived as promised. But the memory of his one failure was never far from his mind.

Chapter 5

He woke, on Thanksgiving morning, with a strong feeling of apprehension. He still wasn't sure if he could handle going home. He had committed though and was never one to shy away from a difficult task.

He decided he would run long and fast today, as that always helped his mood. His iPod in hand he selected his favorite music. He set out, heading for the park. There were a few other runners out and he breezed past them, setting a blistering pace. Running hard he tried to empty his head of all the anxiety that going to see his family was creating. He loved them dearly but lately had been hard-pressed to face the fact that her was now on his own, with no prospect of having a family. By the time he had done one circuit of the lake, he was exhausted and sweaty. He went for a second lap and then headed home at a much slower pace.

Back in his penthouse he put on the coffee machine and checked his phone. Nothing from Ty or Dan. Good, he thought.

Feeling much less apprehensive he stepped into a cooling shower. His leg was bugging him again. Letting the water cascade over his head, he reflected on the past couple of days. Perhaps things were looking up. He seemed to be feeling a bit brighter, his encounter with Christina proof of that. Nonetheless he reminded himself to take things easy.

Towelling off on the way to his bedroom, he caught sight of Vivienne's picture smiling at him from his dresser. He silently kept moving. He chose jeans and a yellow casual shirt, and since the day was quite cool he put on a blue cashmere sweater.

Breakfast at the local diner had seemed like a good idea, but that proved to be a mistake. Entering the diner, he found it difficult to find a seat but spied one over in the corner. Seated, he watched as children busied themselves colouring placemats. He tried to concentrate on the menu over the sounds of happy chatter.

He thought about his upcoming visit to his childhood home.

He'd had a happy childhood. His father bred quarter horses and was very successful at it. Matthew was an accomplished horseman, having learned to ride at an early age. His father still kept Matthew's horse. Vivienne didn't much like horses. This was one thing that he did alone. He surprised himself by realizing that he was looking forward to seeing Phantom, his ornery quarter horse.

On that happy thought he paid his bill, left a tip and went home.

He spent his time texting Ty and Dan. They both reported that things were heating up but that they were not in the line of fire yet. This was good news and it allayed even more of the anxiety he was feeling. Today of all days he did not want to be the bearer of bad news.

Leaving his penthouse shortly after, he settled in for the drive. He fell in with the flow of traffic, all heading, he presumed, to family gatherings for Thanksgiving. Traffic thinned out the closer he got to his destination. He turned onto the road leading to his home, steeling himself for what lay ahead. He began to shut down his feelings. He knew this was going to take a lot of effort on his part. But he approached it like any other mission – with determination.

He pulled up next to his sister Susan's car. Except for the recent texting, he hadn't spoken to her for a long time. No reason really, he just had not felt like it. She always managed to bring up something to do with Vivienne. Determinedly he made his way to the front door, carrying a bouquet for his mother. He entered unnoticed and was greeted by the aroma of turkey. A buzz of conversation came from the back of the house.

The first to notice him was his niece Sara, who came bounding, yelling "Uncle Matt! Oh, goody, goody, you're here!" She grabbed him around his legs and smiled up at him with her blue eyes and freckled nose. Matthew handed the flowers to his Mother with one hand, lifted Sara with the other. She put her arms around his neck and kissed his cheek over and over with big wet kisses. He melted, right then, and held her tight. "Well, glad to see you too, Sara. How's my girlfriend?"

"No! Uncle Matt, I'm not your girlfriend – you're a grown up," she said, kissing him again.

His mother waited her turn to greet him. Shifting Sara to his hip he put his arm round his mother and kissed her on the cheek.

"So glad you came," she said into his ear.

His father extending a hand and Matthew shook it saying, "Good to see you, Dad."

His sister was leaning on the counter.

"Hi Sis, how are things?"

"Great. And you?"

He set Sara down. "Oh, I'm doing OK, I guess."

"What would you like to drink, Matt?" his father asked.

"Scotch, if you have any."

Leaning on the counter next to Susan, crossing his ankles, he forced himself to relax. He had missed a lot lately. His father returned with his drink.

"How's business these days?"

"Good, Dad, we have an operation going on right now. So I may be interrupted. But I hope not, because that would mean it isn't going well."

His mother and sister were busy with dinner, so his father and he went to the living room and talked about the latest brood mare.

Since Vivienne's death, Matthew noticed his dad's difficulty with conversation, his inability to relate, always steering clear of anything to do with Vivienne's death.

The closer it got to dinner the more anxious Matthew became. He was not looking forward to when they would toast one another and say "Happy Thanksgiving."

"Dinner's ready guys."

They took their places at the dining room table. Matthew

pasted on his most pleasant smile as he helped Sara into the chair next to him.

The atmosphere was one of contentment. His mother was in her element, having her family all together once more. Sara was happy to be seated next to Matthew and kept smiling at him as she ate her dinner, encouraged by Matthew to eat her broccoli. Despite the distraction from Sara, Matthew became more anxious with every passing moment waiting for the toast. Sara noticed. She pulled him to her and whispered in his ear, "What's the matter Uncle Matt, are you sad?" He smiled a wan smile and whispered back, "I'm fine Sara, eat your dessert please." He kissed her cheek.

When it came to the part about absent friends his smile left. He raised his wine glass and downed it all at once.

He left the table abruptly, moved with haste to the back door. He slowed when he got there and through eyes blurry with tears saw his cowboy boots sitting under the bench in the mud room. Putting them on, he grabbed his father's barn jacket and went out into the cool fall air. He took a deep breath and walked quickly to the barn. Opening the door, he breathed in deeply. Phantom whinnied a greeting and began shifting around his stall. "Phantom, let's go for a ride."

Matthew saddled and bridled Phantom and led him out of the barn. Phantom was skittish, taking his cue from Matthew, and Matthew wrestled with him for a minute or two then mounted a spinning Phantom.

Stroking the horse's neck, Matthew said in a soothing voice:

"Whoa old fella."

He gathered the reins a little shorter and urged Phantom forward. He responded with a great leap.

Pretty soon they were flying at a full gallop across the field, heading for the entrance to the trail that took them through the woods. Once Phantom had had his head he settled into an easy, more relaxing gait. This was what Matthew liked, being one with his horse, feeling the cool wind on his face. Slowing when they got to the trail, trotting along through the trees, Matthew felt the anxiety dissipate.

As they trotted and sometimes walked along the trail, he reflected on the day, right up until the toast. He needed more of that feeling of love. They reached the river and Matthew pulled Phantom to a stop. He dismounted and settled on a rock close to the shore.

The sound of the fast-moving water calmed Matthew even more and he wondered if there might be someone out there who could make him happy again. He felt so empty, hollowed out. He missed her so much.

When he returned to the house, Sara was outside, playing with the barn cat.

"Uncle Matt, you're back; can I ride on Phantom, please, please?"

Matthew could never say no to her. "Stand on the porch and I'll lift you up here."

He guided Phantom to the steps and was able to lean over far enough to reach Sara.

He placed her in front of him and held her in with his strong arms. Phantom knew he needed to be quiet now and behaved as Matthew urged him into a walk around the yard. Matthew had taken Sara for many rides on Phantom. He taught her to ride as well.

He and Vivienne had often spoken about starting a family. Somehow the timing never seemed right.

"Mummy said you were unhappy because Aunty Vivi was not here and that's why you left us. Where is Aunty Vivi? Is she still in heaven, Uncle Matt?"

Matthew's heart missed a beat. "Yes, Sara, she is still in heaven."

"Good, do you want see her?"

How could he answer that? When she had died, he had wanted to die too. He thought for a minute.

"Yes, Sara, I do, very much."

"Mummy says we will all be together, when we die. Is that right?"

"Oh, I hope so."

"OK Sara, time to put Phantom in his stall." He dismounted and led them to the barn. He lifted Sara and placed her on a hay bale out of the way. He led Phantom into his box and removed the saddle and bridle, gave him some water and hay and a pat on the neck. "Thanks old fella, see you soon."

He lifted Sara down and took her hand, which disappeared inside his. He relished the feel of it, something for him to hang on to.

When they got back the dishes had been cleared. "Sorry I left like that," he said, seeing his mother. She looked at him with sympathy.

He headed for his jacket and took out his phone, it was flashing. "Damn. I should have taken it with me."

Three messages. He read the first one. It was from Dan. *Call me asap*

The second one was Dan again. *Where the hell are you?? Call me*

The third one was from Ty. *Jesus Christ it's all going downhill. Call me*

He speed-dialed Dan, who answered on the first tone.

"Dan, what's happening?"

"Ty says they are under attack by the rebels, we need to get some more resources in there."

"OK, I'm leaving now. See you at the office in about an hour."

He grabbed his jacket turned to his mother. "Something's up, have to go now."

"See you soon."

He ran out the front door and jumped in his Mercedes and sped out of the yard, leaving in a cloud of dust. Once on the highway he kicked it into overdrive and was at the office in forty-five minutes.

He rode the elevator anxiously up to the twentieth floor and strode into the office, meeting Dan just outside his office door.

"Great way to finish Thanksgiving," said Dan.

"What's the status now?"

There was a buzz of activity in the office as the communications guys were working feverishly to re-establish contact with anyone connected with Midnight Security.

"Well, right now we don't know, communications have been cut off for the past half hour."

Matthew opened his office door threw his coat on the couch, took out his phone and called Conrad Hyatt.

Conrad answered anxiously.

"Do you have any sway with the ruling faction, Conrad? We need help over there. My man in charge says he is being overrun by rebels determined to gain control of your oil well."

"I was just speaking with my office in Abyei," Conrad replied. "We can get hold of some reinforcements but not until tonight. I hope they can hang on."

The office was in full military mode as each person was doing their utmost to help.

Dan and Matthew stayed until midnight. Communications were restored within two hours and they finally heard that Ty had his reinforcements. Conrad had been able to procure enough firepower to deter the rebels. They had fought hard, retreating when they realized they were outnumbered. Casualties had been kept to the minimum and none of Midnight Security's personnel had died. Matthew breathed a huge sigh of relief.

"Go home, Dan, apologize to Jane for me and hold her close tonight."

Matthew sat back on his office couch, nursing a scotch. He wished he had someone to call and apologize to. He stayed for a while in the silence of the office.

When he finally left it was close to one a.m. He drove through the quiet streets, parked in his designated parking spot and keyed in the code for the elevator. The doors opened immediately and he punched in the penthouse code. This was the part he disliked lately, no one to hold him in their arms and kiss the hell out of him.

He took a deep breath and opened his door, dropped his keys on the foyer table, took off his coat and headed to the still tidy kitchen.

He was tired and his leg hurt more than usual. The hard ride on Phantom hadn't helped.

He put on pyjama bottoms, returned to the living room, ate a sandwich as he watched the TV and followed it with a third scotch. CNN was reporting on the unrest in Southern Sudan.

Little did they know what was really going on!

He headed to the bedroom, dropping into his bed, hoping for sleep to claim him fast tonight. It did and he dreamed of Vivienne. He saw her smiling face, her blue eyes.

He awoke when it was still dark, aroused. He smiled to himself and lay there remembering all of it. Her memory was so clear he heard her speak and he had seen her smile. He was unable to reach her though. He desperately wanted her back.

"Do you think that nosey journalist got the message when she found Manny?"

"She better have or else we'll have to make sure she does. I followed her home and she was so freaked she didn't even see me."

"Good. We'll just keep our eye on her for now."

"We may want to hear what she's up to in that apartment of hers."

"Let's hold off on that. I think she might just decide to shelve that article. OK, let's split."

Chapter 6

Christina didn't notice the black sedan that cruised by her building. She was too busy trying to decide if she should shelve the article for a while. Truth be told, after seeing him dead, she wasn't as brave as she thought she was. "I can work on something else for a while."

Work on something else? she thought. All I see are emerald eyes.

She had not been at all productive since the lecture. She smiled to herself remembering how bold she had been introducing herself like that. She wondered what she had been thinking.

Thanksgiving, had come and gone, with no article. She had spent time with her friends, but that had not been as much fun as in other years. She even called up her favorite male friend. That proved a disaster as well. He had not been impressed with her distant attitude and had left, frustrated that he could not keep her attention no matter how skilled his lovemaking was.

Besides worrying about her safety and wondering how Matthew Bryson had spent his Thanksgiving, she was almost ready to write herself off.

Matthew Bryson, on the other hand, felt that he was making progress with his new take-charge attitude. He was going to let a little light into his life and he would let the chips fall where they may. He was fed up with feeling so lifeless – this was not him. In fact, he had been amused when she had appeared beside him. It was obvious that she was attracted to him and judging by the slight tremble he felt when shaking her hand, and that she appeared a bit unsteady on her feet, she could be someone he might like to get to know a little bit. She didn't seem like a silly girl – after all she was a journalist and as Dan pointed out, they were a brave lot. He liked that in a woman. He did not go for the clingy type.

Dan noticed a change in him. He didn't know what had brought it about but he was pleased for his dearest friend. It had been painful watching him over the past year. Gone was the happy, carefree, always up for a laugh man he had been used to. He and Jane had tried hard to alleviate some of his grief by inviting him to their house for a barbeque or a dinner or including him on an outing to the movies but it became obvious that none of these things was going to help. The number of times Matt declined became more frequent as time went on and so they stopped asking him. Now, Dan saw a glimmer of hope for his partner and best friend.

"Alright, I know who I can contact for this, Jack. When's the deadline?"

Christina was working on an article that she hoped would bring attention to the growing problem of human trafficking in the city. The dead informant had been promising to give her names of some of the more prominent people controlling the prostitutes. Now, she had a more pressing project as Jack had given her just a week to submit her article.

Smiling, she made more coffee and prepared a bagel and cream cheese. She silently mouthed, "Thank you, *In the Know Magazine*."

She made the phone call and after being given the run around, finally got an appointment at four the day after tomorrow.

The next two days she was occupied with her research on the subject.

"Your four o'clock is here, Mr. Bryson."

"Already? Thanks, Anne. You can send her in. What was her name again?"

When she told him and he remembered who she was, he smirked.

"Good afternoon, Ms. Melville. We must stop making a habit of this." He held out his hand. She shook it with the same firm grip that had taken him by surprise the first time.

He noticed her flushed face as he indicated to the couch. "Please be seated."

"Thank you."

"Can I get you anything to drink?"

"No, I'm good. Thanks for seeing me. I know you must be busy."

No sooner were the words out of her mouth than his Blackberry buzzed on the desk beside him. He retrieved it and checked the caller ID and let it go to voice mail.

"Sorry about that. Now, what kind of information can I give you? You do know there are lots of things I can't discuss, don't you?"

"I'll take my chances. What kind of security does your company provide?"

"We provide surveillance and counter-surveillance. Close protection training, secure transportation, and personal security. We operate in several countries."

"How did you get started?"

"When I left the military, shortly after 9/11. I saw how 9/11 changed the way security was viewed and that the world would never be the same again. I was still relatively young and with my business partner we put this company together in 2008. We started small, providing personal security, mostly here in America, but as our reputation grew so did our clientele. We are still small, in the grand scheme of things. This was a natural fit for us."

Christina continued with her questions.

Matthew watched, noting her ability to ask relevant questions, and was impressed with her intelligence, to say nothing of her beauty.

"Can you tell me how successful you have been? I mean, do you always succeed?"

Matthew shifted uncomfortably in his chair. His jaw tightened momentarily. He recovered fast and answered, "Yes, but there are always degrees of success. Nothing is one hundred percent a sure thing. There are too many variables in the security business."

She went back to her apartment and began to write the article while it was fresh in her mind.

She was perturbed by the fact that he kept invading her thoughts and her deadline was less than week away, but with supreme effort she managed it.

Hitting send just before the deadline, she relaxed. When the article was published, maybe she would call him to get his reaction!

The phone interrupted Matthew in the middle of a proposal he was writing, and he reached for it absentmindedly.

"Matthew Bryson, may I help you?"

"Mr. Bryson, Christina Melville. The article was published today thought you might like a copy." Her words were tumbling out of her mouth.

"What? Oh! Ms. Melville I'm sorry, I didn't catch all of that." After a silence she continued more slowly.

"The article is in this month's edition. I wondered if you had a copy or if I could bring one over to you." She held her breath.

"Well sure. No, I don't have a copy. I'm here all day."

"Great, I'll see you soon then." She hung up and heaved a sigh.

Yeeessss...

Matthew sat back in his chair. He smiled and wondered where this was going. A half hour later, Christina entered his office. His smile disarmed her and nearly made her trip.

"That didn't take long," he said, coming around his desk. "Good to see you again, Ms. Melville. Please have a seat." He indicated to the couch. Sitting, she removed the magazine from her bag and set it on the table in front of her. Placing her hands in her lap she looked directly at him and waited expectantly. He looked at her with a slight gleam in his eyes.

She shifted, straightening her coat as she said, "I hope you approve of the article. I tried to be as accurate as I could."

He bent down in front of her and retrieved the magazine. She caught a hint of his aftershave; *CK Obsession*, she thought. He straightened and turned, returning to his desk, flipping pages.

With his back to her she made a hasty assessment: *Great ass!* "Page forty-five," she said once he was seated.

He looked up and noted her flushed cheeks and slightly parted full lips.

"Right, here it is."

While he was reading the opening paragraph she continued her assessment: Chestnut hair (slightly unruly), strong broad shoulders, long, well-manicured fingers, great suit, perfectly matching silk tie...

He looked up fully aware that she had been checking him out. Light sparkling in his eyes and unable to contain his smile, he said, "Well, this first piece is great! I'll read the rest later. Now, Ms. Melville... may I call you Christina?"

Through a smile she answered, "Of course, Matthew."

"Well, now that that's out of the way what are you doing for lunch?"

She swallowed hard and replied, "Nothing, I was planning on returning home to work on my next project."

"Good, then grab your purse and let's go eat."

Walking behind her, grinning to himself, it was his turn now. Taking inventory of her assets he noted: tall and slender, long curly hair... can't tell if she has a nice ass... shapely legs, great boots. He imagined she had a hot body beneath her long coat. He really hadn't noticed much on the other occasions they had come across each other, except to note she was very charismatic and not hard to look at. He hadn't been in a good place then but definitely had a much better outlook these past couple of weeks.

They arrived at the restaurant and found a table. After placing their order Christina took the initiative and started the conversation.

"When I met you in the bar you told me you lived quite close by. So where do you live?"

"I have a place in the Bentley Tower on the north side of town. How about you?"

"Nowhere that grand; my apartment is in the south end on Grafton Street."

The conversation continued and her bold behaviour was paying off as she felt relaxed and comfortable in his company. She only hoped he hadn't thought of her as pushy, but it was he that asked her to lunch, wasn't it?

She learned that he was ex-Navy Seal, he liked to run, was a horseman and had a sister.

On the other hand, Christina didn't divulge much about herself, sticking to her journalistic accomplishments, mostly. She did tell him of her Grav Maga training, though, and he seemed to be quite impressed with that revelation.

He drove her back to her car.

Not wanting this to be over, she thanked him for lunch, sounding far more cheerful than she felt. She wanted to kiss him goodbye but she was pretty sure that would definitely be too bold and even pushy. She left it as it was and climbed out waving to him as she unlocked her car. On the way home she convinced herself that that was probably the only meal she would share with him and resigned herself to that fact.

She didn't see the black sedan three cars behind her.

Back in her apartment she sat for a long time reflecting on her luncheon, wondering if it had just been an impulse on his part to break up his work day. He flirted with her, didn't he? Well, she had satisfied her curiosity to a certain point. He was every bit as handsome and charismatic as she knew he would be. Now it was time to move on, she had work to do. She wasn't even sure that he could be trusted.

Chapter 7

Matthew was glad he had acted on impulse. She was delightful to talk to and he liked the way she drew her tongue across her lips before taking a mouthful of her food. He thought her lipstick was very attractive, a perfect shade to enhance her very sexy mouth. It certainly set his mind wandering. Distracted, he returned to the proposal he had abandoned before lunch.

By the time he had finished it was late.

Matthew leant back in his chair and looked out over the city. The lights were just starting to twinkle in the dusk. It was getting dark earlier these days. He had survived Thanksgiving. Just! Christmas didn't seem that far away now.

At the bar once again, favorite drink set before him, he watched Harry moving quietly, going about his duties. The soft clink of glasses being loaded in the washer was the only sound penetrating Matthew's brain. Though he struggled to push her from his thoughts, Vivienne kept creeping in. How was he going to move on?

His brain swirled with thoughts of her, thoughts of his love for her, how he still missed her more than he could ever say. How every time he's at his lowest, he only has to close his eyes and she is there smiling, kissing him, making him fearless.

Matthew sipped on his second scotch.

"Bye for now, Harry. I probably won't be seeing as much of you from now on." He put on his coat and left the bar. He had one more thing to do when he got back to his penthouse and he was not sure if he could do it.

Entering his apartment, he hesitated for just a second before entering his bedroom. He stopped in front of the dresser and stared at Vivienne's picture. Sitting on the edge of his bed, breathing increased and his heart rate rose. He took a deep, steadying breath.

"The love I have for you will not go away; it will always be there. It should have been the two of us forever."

He took another deep breath and held it. He exhaled and took hold of the photo and held it to his chest. Standing, he headed to his walk-in closet, and managed to find the memory box that he placed on the top shelf almost a year ago. It contained her engagement ring and their wedding bands, as well as the love notes she had always managed to conceal in his uniform when he was deployed.

He took the memory box down, nearly dropping it as he fumbled with the clasp. His eyes fixed on his wedding band. He picked it up, caressing it between his finger and thumb. Titanium, indestructible, wasn't that supposed to be how their love was? He took a final, long look at her picture.

Chapter 8

He was seated in his comfy office chair. It had been a few days since he had pulled the memory box off the shelf. He found the copy of *In the Know Magazine* underneath some papers on his desk. Due to other commitments, he hadn't gotten around to finishing the article. He moved to his couch, asked Anne to bring him a coffee and began reading. She had written a thoughtful and informative article. He liked her style. In fact, he not only liked her journalism style but wouldn't mind seeing her again. She had managed to see beyond his company and had described him as a CEO with high moral standards a great sense of empathy and justice, someone wanting to help keep the world a safer place.

When she answered the buzzer, he said, "Hi, I'm glad you're home." Her breath caught in her throat and she stared at the security camera image. She thought she was hallucinating but then he turned toward the camera and smiled. *(Oh my God, It's him!!)* Here he was on her doorstep.

"Ye... Yes I'm home," she stuttered. "W-what... are you doing here?"

"Are you going to let me up or do I have to have a conversation over the intercom?"

"Yes, of course, sorry." She hit the buzzer then ran to the bedroom and looked in the mirror: hell, she was not prepared for a guest, especially not him!

She hoped he was taking the stairs, as that would give her time to at least run a brush through her hair and slap on some lipstick. The doorbell rang just as she got the lipstick out, "Just a minute," she yelled, putting it on hastily.

After taking a deep breath and straightening her top, she walked to the door. He filled the doorway. He had one hand leaning on the door frame and was smiling the most charming smile she had ever seen. And those eyes were just glinting with amusement.

"About time! I thought you had changed your mind."

He waited a moment and then another. His smile slid away. "Can I come in," he said, looking expectantly past her, "or do you have company?"

Incapable of saying anything at the moment, she stepped back and ushered him in. He stood just inside the door holding the magazine. His aftershave wafted past her nose. She gestured toward her living room. "Follow me."

Clearing away papers from her coffee table, she asked, "Why are you here?"

"May I?" He gestured toward the chair.

"Oh sure have a seat! Here, why don't you take off your coat." He set the magazine down and handed her his coat. She was recovering from the shock a bit now. She hung his leather jacket on the bar stool.

He sat all the while, following her movement.

Christina noted the glint in his bright shining eyes. His mouth slightly upturned at the corners.

"I took a chance you might be home. I finished reading your article and wanted to congratulate you for doing such a good job. It was a very thoughtful and insightful piece. I am impressed."

Christina blushed and said, smiling, "Thank you, Matthew, I don't usually get a personal visit to congratulate me."

"Well then there's always a first time, right?"

"Would you like a glass of wine? Merlot or Sauvignon Blanc?" Then remembering that she had seen him drink scotch she said, "I do have some single malt."

"I like a girl with a well-stocked bar. Scotch please."

Retrieving the scotch bottle from the top shelf, she poured him one and handed it to him. Their fingers touched briefly. He took the tumbler from her and waited for her to come back with her wine.

Seated opposite him on the couch she raised her glass, "Cheers! Thanks for the compliment."

She watched him take a sip.

"How did you know where to find me?"

He laughed and his face lit up again, "Remember you told me Grafton Street? Well, I used my own resources!"

She took a gulp of her wine. "Right, should have known; nothing's secret anymore is it?"

"Not in the world we know today."

He was beginning to enjoy the evening and was quite certain that she was as well. They fell into an easy conversation about the state of the world. Retrieving the magazine and opening it to her article he referred to some of her observations. "Here," he said, pointing to one paragraph where she talked about the threat of homegrown terrorism. "You're right to suggest that private security is going to become more and more relevant as the threats increase."

She renewed her wine, having consumed it rather too fast, perhaps. He refused another scotch, as he was driving.

Later, when it turned more personal, he noted she was adept at diverting attention from herself. She was proving to be quite a mystery.

His thoughts turned to her very kissable lips, noting that even though he had arrived unexpectedly she still looked fantastic. Certain he had made the right decision, he decided to jump in with both feet.

"Do you run at all?"

"What? Run. Yes I do, why?"

"Well I like to run and maybe we could go together on Saturday if the weather cooperates." He held his breath.

She didn't reply right away. She was trying to play it cool.

"I think that would be a great idea."

He exhaled. "OK. How about we meet at Rockwood Park entrance at eight a.m. Do you know how to get there? It's a great place to run."

"I do. By the way, I don't have your cell number, in case of the weather, you know. I don't think you have mine, do you?"

"No, I don't."

"Good, because I think that would have been too creepy."

They entered each other's number in their phones and then Matthew rose and retrieved his coat. Shrugging into his jacket he picked up the magazine and headed for the door. Christina followed. She placed her hand on his forearm to halt him for just a second.

"Thanks for coming," she said. "I'll see you Saturday, weather permitting."

He looked directly into her eyes. "I'm glad I did. See you on Saturday."

Leaving her building, preoccupied with thoughts of seeing her again, he passed by a black sedan on the way to his car, failing to notice that the occupant had taken a picture of him as he passed under the street lamp.

Christina closed the door and leaned heavily on it.

Grinning like a fool she let out a silent whistle. Saturday seemed like a long ways away.

She heard her mantra: proceed with caution. It had always been her preferred mode d'emploi. She didn't seem to be listening.

Saturday she was up early. She donned her running gear and checked the weather. It said sunny, cold, slight chance of rain in the morning. She packed her gym bag with her windbreaker and some extra clothes, a habit she had had for a while, having been caught in a downpour while running before.

She tied her hair back in a ponytail, put on her running shoes and fleece jacket. She left her apartment in plenty of time to get there before he did.

Matthew pulled in to the parking area and saw with some relief that Christina's Escape was already there. He had spent the days before wondering if he should have suggested this run. Now that he was here he was glad he had and smiled to himself as he drew up beside her. She got out of her car and smiled, her dark eyes dancing in anticipation. "Hello, great day for a run don't you think?" Again she noted his broad shoulders under his jacket.

"Yes, I hope we don't get that rain they forecast. Which way should we go?" She looked every bit the experienced runner, dressed the way she was.

"You're more familiar with this place, so what's your preferred route?"

"Are you up for a real work out or just a leisurely run?"

"I could do with a good run. I've been lazy lately."

He was delighted with her answer.

Old habits were hard to break. His competitive spirit surfaced.

They warmed up with a few stretching exercises and he led the way, giving her the chance to admire his physique. She fell into step and was soon running at a steady pace beside him. He led them through the woods and up the hill that overlooked the golf course. On the way up he increased his speed, just to see if she could keep up. She did and to his surprise she passed him about half way up the hill. When she reached the summit she looked back at him laughing and told him to "Hurry up." Grinning, he arrived at the top and congratulated her then took off without warning down the other side of the hill while calling back to her, "Race you to the bottom."

"Not fair!" She took off after him, but he managed to keep ahead of her this time and when she arrived at the bottom only seconds after him he caught her round the waist to slow her progress, as she was in danger of going out of control. He spun her round and halted his spin planting his foot firmly on the ground. She was laughing and then she had her arms around his neck for balance. Their faces were inches apart. Her heart skipped a beat and she stopped before she took advantage of the situation. His expression made her wonder if he was doing the same thing. Clearing his throat, he released his grip on her and said, "Come on, not too much farther. It's starting to look a bit ominous."

She felt the first drops. He quickened his pace. "There's a shelter just round this curve," he said. She caught up to him and they ran into the small lean-to. They were panting by now and drawing deep breaths. He drew her to him to get her out of the rain. She was so close to him now. Leaning into him, she brushed her lips over his. He remained still and she took that as a yes. She deepened her kiss and he responded fluttering his tongue over her lips. Her blood was pounding in her head and she could not help herself. She grabbed his bottom lip gently between her teeth and he pulled her closer. His body was hot, as was hers. He continued to hold her against him even after she stopped kissing him.

Christina noted the troubled expression that slid briefly across his face. She wondered if she had been too forward. She stepped back. "Uh, I'm sorry I should not have done that."

"No, it was me. Let's get out of here," he replied hastily.

The rain eased and they continued their run. Gone was the playful Matthew replaced with one who reminded her of the night when they had first met.

Back to their vehicles, he returned to his lighthearted demeanor. "Well that was great, maybe we can do it again soon?"

Christina was not sure how to answer. She had hoped he would invite her for breakfast somewhere. "Well, I guess I need to head home and work on an article. The run was a good idea, I think."

Just as she was opening her car door, Matthew turned her toward him and said, "Back in the shelter... I really liked that... I'm just not used to women who are that bold." He grinned. "Besides, it's been a long time. I think I'm out of practice." Leaning in to her and putting his hand behind her head, pulling her face to his, he kissed her hard. "There! Now I feel like I am in charge." There was a twinkle in his eye and he had a most endearing little smirk where the corner of his mouth twitched upward.

Christina steadied herself on the car door, looked at him and said, "I'm sorry but I'm sort of a 'take charge girl' – not one of my better traits."

"Well," he said, "I'm a sort of a 'take charge guy', how's that?"

"I don't know." Her body was singing; she felt hot and her hands were tingling.

"Breakfast?"

"What, like this?" She pointed between them

"Well?" He looked at her expectantly.

Her gaze fell on her sport bag. Her face brightened as it dawned on her.

On his way back to his apartment, Matthew was only half concentrating on his driving, and almost ran the red light. Pulling into his parking spot he switched off his engine and leaned back. At no time in the past year had he imagined he would be doing this. She was unsettling him. He had it all under control until he came across her. He had become aware of the fact that since he had visited her apartment, he had not felt the same deep sadness. He felt more optimistic these past few days. In fact, he had to admit to himself, that he got quite excited at the prospect of seeing her today. He smiled to himself remembering how surprised he was. Who would have thought that she could have beaten him up that hill! He was unable to resist pulling her to him. It had triggered a response in him that he had not felt for what seemed like a lifetime. He didn't know how this would end. He was willing to try. After all he was the adventurous type, wasn't he? Looking up into his rear-view mirror he saw the Escape approaching. He waited until she opened her door and then he got out. With a wry smile she said, "Driving could use a bit of improvement. Do you always stop that suddenly? Running red lights can be dangerous you know."

He liked her humor. "Sorry, I'm usually better than that but I was distracted."

She fell in step with him as they moved towards the elevator. He keyed in the code and stepped back to let her enter, moving to the panel he entered the penthouse code, all the time keeping his gaze on her.

She became uncomfortably warm, she trembled at the thought of him kissing her or doing God knows what to her.

Opening his door, Matthew took a breath as he entered. He had not had another woman in here since Vivienne. Motioning for her to put her bag down, he asked if she would like coffee.

He was heading for the kitchen as Christina replied, "I would love one. Thanks." She surveyed her surroundings as she followed him down the hall to the living area, noting that he had very good taste in furniture. While he was preparing the coffee, she moved to the window. The floor-to-ceiling windows afforded a spectacular view all the way to the coast, where she could see the harbour. From thirty floors up the rain clouds scudding past seemed quite low.

Musing to herself, she folded her arms across her chest.

Matthew turned and observed her reflection in the window. She had a look on her face that he could not quite determine. She looked, what? Reflective! Wondering if he should have invited her to use his shower, he moved over to her and stood beside her. "Great view isn't it. I especially like it at sunset."

He had removed his fleece and was wearing just a t-shirt and track pants. His body was well proportioned and he obviously took care of it. His arms were tanned and hard, with a dusting of fine hair, bleached blond by the sun. They looked powerful; she was sure he could lift her with one hand. His t-shirt emphasized a nice set of abs as well. She bet his long legs were as well developed as the rest of him. Hard to tell with his track pants on. He was barefoot and that sort of turned her on too.

Hearing the coffee percolator buzz, he found an excuse to move away from her. He was having a hard time resisting the urge to grab her and kiss her. It was all starting to feel right even if he hadn't known her for more than what seemed like a few minutes.

He set out two mugs and poured. It occurred to him that this was a real learning curve and he thought it was going to be interesting discovering things about her. He suddenly needed to know everything, because for sure he didn't know a thing past the fact she was bold, beautiful and a pretty good journalist.

"Coffee's ready, how do you take yours?"

"Milk only, thanks."

They sat on the bar stools next to each other and she smiled. "This is reminiscent of the first time I saw you, isn't it?"

"Yes, it is, I remember looking at you and all I could see were your beautiful eyes."

"Funny, I did the same," she laughed. He thought of angels then.

They fell silent, leisurely drinking their coffee, both with their own thoughts.

Eventually they had finished and Matthew said, "If we are going for breakfast we had better get a move on." As he grinned, it made his eyes sparkle once more. "I think it is going to be brunch now, anyway."

Pushing away from the breakfast bar and helping Christina off the stool he brushed a kiss over her cheek. She turned and couldn't stop herself. She kissed him on his mouth, looking at him all the while. His brow twitched slightly but he returned the kiss, lightly touching and teasing her lips gently with his tongue.

Christina pulled away first and, exhaling slowly, gently blocked his advance, placing her hands flat on his chest. She felt his hard sculpted pectoral muscles hot beneath her palms. "Where is your shower?" she said fast as she moved towards the hallway to retrieve her bag.

Matthew checked himself; he let her pass, saying, "Here, this way," and pointed to his bedroom.

Christina followed. She noted the king-size bed, still unmade. The en-suite bathroom was enormous, with a spa shower, the likes of which she had never seen before. There were at least six jets placed at various levels down the walls. A large copper bath tub was at one end, and there was a vanity with two sinks, and a wall mirror that extended the width of the bathroom. A toilet was discreetly placed behind a frosted-glass petition. The whole place had the feel of a Roman spa. Matthew followed her in and removed a large white towel from the linen closet, placing it on the heated towel rail, above the chair next to the shower.

"I hope you find everything you need."

"I think I will be fine"

He turned and walked out, closing the door behind him.

He let out a sigh and stood by the windows, staring out over the city.

She fascinated him. She was bold and brave and mysterious. He had felt the electricity that passed between them; she had set him on fire with that kiss, and he would have continued if she hadn't stopped him. He knew she felt it as well. The slight tremble he had felt from her hands when she touched his chest...

He heard the shower turn on.

Standing in the shower, letting the water cascade over her, she too wondered how this whole thing was going to develop. During their run she had been pleasantly surprised at his almost playful attitude, certainly compared to his demeanor from their first meeting. He was puzzling though. She hoped that he would enlighten her one day soon. There she was, thinking of the future already. Could she trust him?

She returned to the living room dressed in jeans and a black shirt, her hair damp and curly; she had no makeup on.

Matthew thought she looked very sexy.

"That is a great shower. I almost didn't want to get out." Her almond eyes were bright and when she smiled they lit up.

"I like it too; it takes away the aches and pains."

Matthew moved away from the window, heading to the bedroom, removing his t-shirt on the way and affording her a look at his well-developed back. "I won't be long," he said over his shoulder as he entered the bedroom.

When he returned he was dressed in black jeans and a charcoal sport shirt that complimented his eyes. He came over to her and she caught a hint of his body wash. "We clean up well don't we!"

"Oh yes you do, don't you!"

"Come on let's go. I'm hungry; aren't you?"

She grabbed her gym bag and they headed out to the elevator.

Leaving the underground parking lot, he had to drive past a black sedan parked close to the entrance.

"Wish people wouldn't park so close to the entrance, makes it hard to get out."

They arrived at the same diner where he had had breakfast on Thanksgiving. It was almost as busy; nevertheless, they found a table in the corner. He felt much happier this time and grinned at her.

"What?" she said, arching her eyebrows.

"Oh, nothing. I was just thinking that I'm having a really nice time."

"So am I. What do you recommend?" she said looking at the menu.

He studied her intently. She was getting under his skin for sure.

"I recommend the waffles with fresh fruit and whipped cream... if you like that kind of thing."

"Do we need all those calories?"

He winked, a mischievous look on his face. "We may."

She stared back at him. Her heart skipped and she was wondering if she was reading more into that statement than she should. *Oh my!*

He ordered an egg-white omelet and she went for the waffles.

He took that as a positive sign.

"How long have you been a freelance journalist?" he asked, sipping his coffee.

"Nearly five years now," she replied. The conversation continued. Matthew pushed her for details about her life. She was cautious in her replies, divulging very little, but he did learn that she had lived in a lot of different places.

They hardly noticed as the diner began to empty. Matthew placed his hand over hers and felt the heat radiate. She looked over at him and he asked, "Would you come back to my place? The sun sets earlier now and we could see what it's like today..." His voice had become slightly hoarse.

She felt she was falling under his spell. "I would like that very much."

Once back in his apartment she saw how large it really was. It was designed with an open concept, like a loft, with dark hardwood floors leading to a breakfast bar that separated the kitchen and living area. There were gleaming granite countertops, brushed aluminum appliances. The living area contained a comfortable couch – '*Stressless*', she thought – an ottoman, and an armchair. The flat screen TV dominated the wall opposite with a gas fireplace recessed beneath. In front of it was a beautiful Persian rug. The overall effect was monochromatic except for the cherry red couch. The armchair was black and the Persian rug matched both perfectly.

To chase away the chill, Matthew lit the fire with the hand control and invited her to sit. Settling, Christina found it hard to control the trembling that seemed to occur every time he was close by.

"What kinds of music do you like?" He was standing in front of the fireplace. She looked up at him. She didn't think she would ever get used to his eyes. The electricity between them was almost palpable.

"Bach, Beethoven, Indie, Josh Groban, The Killers, all kinds really."

He loaded the sound system, picking up the hand control as he moved to the couch and pressing play on the way. He settled at the other end. All he really wanted to do was sit close to her. He was becoming seriously undone. Music was piped throughout the apartment and the effect was magnificent. They were literally surrounded by it.

Christina was staring into the flames, deep in thought.

Matthew was studying her, wondering what she was feeling, if it was anything akin to how he felt.

Christina's mind raced. She had never experienced this before and wasn't sure she could handle any of it. Her life had been almost devoid of love. She had bounced around from foster home to foster home, always in the hope that she would be adopted. By the time she was thirteen she realized that that was probably not going to happen. She learned to accept her lot in life and at age eighteen was kicked loose from the system and essentially left to fend for herself. Now she wanted to be held by him, feel his strong body against hers. She wanted love and she was willing to take a chance.

Matthew interrupted her thoughts. Crossing his ankle over his knee he faced her, stroking his finger down her cheek, raising goosebumps all over her body.

"You know what? We've shared a lunch and a breakfast, so how about we share a supper as well?

"What, you mean here, or we go out again?"

"We could order in; it's early yet, and I have a drawer full of take-out menus."

"Well, after watching the sunset," she said, "maybe we can go out for dinner. I know a place on the south side. Greek. You like that?"

He smiled and felt a surge of relief that she had not rejected his idea. He would have said yes to any restaurant she suggested. Time slipped by as they got to know each other a little better. He got up and went towards the windows, pressing the button on yet another remote. The electric blinds rose slowly, revealing the cityscape all the way to the ocean.

The view was spectacular in the evening light. He went

back to the couch and held out his hand: "Come with me," he said in a slightly husky voice.

He led her to the windows and stood behind her with his hands on her shoulders. Leaning his head on hers he felt the softness of her curls brushing his cheek.

She let a small gasp escape.

Matthew moved beside her. "How's that for making good on my promise?"

"Breathtaking, Matthew. Isn't it beautiful?"

"Yes you are," he whispered

Leaving her side, he headed to his bar. He needed a bit more space in order to collect himself.

"Glass of wine?" he asked her, opening the Merlot.

"Yes please."

Standing in front of the windows they finished their wine. He put his arm around her waist and they watched the sun set, the skyline silhouetted against the deepening red and orange.

"OK," he said. "Show me your side of town."

"Put your keys away," she said. "I'll drive this time and I'll drop you back afterwards."

This was different!

"But I need to change and put on some make-up. We can swing by my place. That's if you don't mind."

"I don't mind at all but I think you look great just the way you are."

Christina watched him as they made their way to the parking level, wondering if things were moving too fast. He seemed ill at ease all of a sudden. A shadow, which she interpreted as doubt, passed briefly over his face. Perhaps this was too good to be true.

She only hoped he would let her down easy. She had been down that road before. She was no stranger to disappointment. Nevertheless, she was going to let this play out tonight.

At Christina's building the elevator was in use so they took the stairs two at a time. They were both panting slightly by the time they arrived at her door, but they entered laughing.

Christina came to a sudden halt. "Is everything all right?" Matthew asked.

"What? Oh yes I'm fine," she answered distractedly. "Come on in."

They walked to the living room. She flicked the light on. "Make yourself at home. I'll only be a minute. Scotch is in the cupboard by the window, top shelf, help yourself." He opened a few cupboards looking for a glass, poured a drink and settled on the couch. Looking around he noted there were no family pictures anywhere. Unusual, he thought. Perhaps they were in the bedroom.

Putting his glass on the coaster on her end table he absentmindedly straightened the lampshade.

She called from the bedroom, "Did you find a glass? I'm nearly ready."

She returned transformed, wearing a wool sapphire blue dress, with a plunging neckline that accentuated her curvy body. Her black stockings and Jimmy Choo, take charge, knee-high boots with three-inch heels accentuated her long slender legs.

She had managed to put her hair up in a most becoming way.

With a sharp intake of breath Matthew couldn't help the look of surprise that came over him. He cleared his now dry throat, took another sip of his scotch and said, noting her glossy full lips, "You look amazing. Love the boots." Her face flushed and she smiled at him (she'd been doing a lot of that today) "Thank you. I couldn't go out with you, dressed the way I was." His approval had been her intention.

Matthew got up and as he walked with her to the hall closet, he caught a hint of jasmine, which he had smelled when he had seen her at the lecture. He helped her with her cashmere coat. She took one more look over her shoulder on the way out.

Seated next to each other in the booth in the corner of the restaurant, Matthew felt at ease, his doubts allayed. For now, anyway. It took great restraint, but he resisted touching her. He had not felt this way for a whole year. What he could only describe as a lump of ice had resided within him, but he felt himself starting to thaw. He had forgotten how it could be.

He ordered veal masala, she ordered stuffed grape leaves.

Dessert and coffee followed. So did more doubt.

"Matthew, is there something troubling you? You seem distracted. I hope I haven't made you uncomfortable."

He raised his troubled eyes and reached for her hand.

"To tell the truth, Christina, I don't know if I should be leading you on like this."

She stiffened and pulled her hand away. Her face crumpled. "Are you married? Because if you are, tell me now. I don't do mistress."

Dismayed that he had caused her such anguish, Matthew answered hastily: "Not anymore."

She relaxed slightly. "Divorced then?"

"No, widowed." His expression was one of pain.

"Oh... I'm sorry." She thought he was far too young to have to go through that. She didn't ask any more questions, hoping he would elaborate. He seemed unable or unwilling to.

After a long silence, he said, in a low, almost whispering voice, "Her name was Vivienne... she died a year ago."

"Was that why you looked so sad, the first time I saw you?"

"At the bar that night, it was the anniversary of her death. That's why I was so distracted."

Leaning back, she tried to analyze what was happening. He was obviously attracted to her and that must be what had precipitated his statement.

She leaned across, looking into his green eyes, seeing his look of apprehension and a certain amount of fear. She smiled and said, "Lead on, who could resist those eyes," and kissed him gently on the cheek. He smiled and the laugh lines enhanced the light that shone behind his eyes.

He had been holding his breath for what seemed like an eternity. He sighed.

They held each other's gaze. He kissed her.

Matthew paid the bill, left an outrageous tip and helped Christina with her coat as he escorted her out of the restaurant, his step a little lighter.

She said she would drive and he acquiesced, amused at her insistence, wondering if she was always this bossy. She smiled all the way back to Bentley Towers. Parking by the entrance, she turned off the ignition and waited a second or two. Now, they had some clarification on what could only be called the beginning of a new relationship. She had never actively pursued any man before. This one was different. Matthew had demonstrated a tolerance for her forthrightness. So far, anyway.

He leaned over the console and pulled her to him. "Thank you for a lovely evening and the ride; I could have got a cab you know."

"I know, but this is more fun, don't you think?"

"Definitely," he pushed a stray lock of her hair behind her ear and turning her head towards him he kissed her again. He noted her glossy full lips. "I'm going to say good night now. Thank you," he said.

Somewhat surprised at this decision, she felt disappointed. *What the hell! What has changed between the restaurant and here?*

"Good night, Christina." He shut the door and hurried through the entrance without even looking back.

Christina sat there, staring after him. Had she misunderstood him earlier? She headed home in turmoil. Once in her apartment she noticed the tumbler he had left on the end table, picking it up she took it to the sink all the time thinking that the day had begun promisingly but had ended disappointingly. Her eyes misted over. She washed the glass and made her way to her bedroom. After putting on her fuzziest pyjamas she curled up in her bed and wondered how she had, once again, been dealt a load of disappointment. She had wanted him to go further, she was aching for his touch, for some release of her pent-up desire. Resigning herself to the disappointment she closed her eyes but all she saw were his. He had such a kind face and mesmerizing eyes. How could he be so cruel?

She was wallowing in self-pity vowing to forget him by morning. Who needs him anyway? Trying to sleep, she thought she heard her Blackberry ping. She ignored it but sometime later she heard it again. She got up in a daze and went to her purse. Removing her Blackberry, she saw his name pop up twice. She ignored it without even looking at the message. Did she want to answer that now? No, so she shut it off and threw it back into her purse, went to the bathroom then returned to bed, miserable. She was sure his text would be one of those, "I'm sorry, but we can't see each other anymore" messages. How could someone who seemed so brave be such a coward and break off with her that way, when it seemed they had only just begun.

Sleep eluded her. She tossed and turned and cried and wondered how she could feel this devastated over someone she really didn't know.

In the midst of her sorrow, her apartment buzzer sounded. *What now?* Someone ringing the wrong apartment? She pulled the pillow over her head and hoped they would realize their mistake. After the third time she got out of bed, angry that she couldn't even wallow in self-pity without being interrupted. Padding to the door she pressed the intercom. "Wrong apartment," she yelled into it.

"Christina, it's me."

She caught her breath and her heart started racing.

Pressing the intercom again, she said, "Go away you have the wrong apartment."

"Christina, for Christ sake, turn on the video, it's me."

She hesitated. Taking a deep breath before she pressed the video button, staring into the monitor, she saw his distraught face staring back at her.

"Matthew, go away. I get it, you changed your mind." She managed to say it without crying.

"Please let me explain. It's not that at all. Please just let me in," he whispered.

"No. I will read your texts tomorrow when I feel better."

"Read them now, please. I'll wait here all night if I have to."

She turned from the monitor. Leaning on the wall she closed her eyes.

After a few minutes she relented. Whatever it was, she would rather have him tell her face to face. She turned back to the monitor. He looked dishevelled and more anxious than she had ever seen anyone look.

She hit the buzzer and an expression of relief passed over his face as he threw open the door.

She hesitated, before opening the door. He was panting hard, his jaw was tight and his face held an apologetic expression. He threw his arms around her and swept her backwards, taking her by surprise. He kissed her hard and said against her mouth, "I'm sorry, I'm sorry, I need to explain." He pushed back and looked into her face inquiringly, "You read my texts then?"

She pushed him away, hard enough for him to have to take a step to gain his balance. "No," she said, close to tears, her eyes shining. "Why would I do that when I want you to stop being a coward and tell me face to face?"

He looked stunned. Collecting himself he said, "Where is your phone? In here?" He reached for her purse, found her phone. "Password protected?"

"Yes."

He shoved it at her and she entered it with shaking hands. He snatched it back and opened his first text. Holding it up in front of her face:

OMG I'm an idiot please let me explain can I call you?

She read it and looked up at him, saw anxiety written all over his face waiting for her to say something. When she didn't he took it back and scrolled to the next text. she read:

I'm coming over now I haven't changed my mind. I lost it.

She stared at him and relief flooded through her. She stepped toward him and flung her arms around him. He held her and said, "I got scared. I'm a mess as you can see. Who would want to get involved with this?" He clung to her and caressed her. He kissed her passionately and she returned his passion. He could no longer deny what both of them knew was a fact. She felt so comfortable, she was soft and sensual and he realized that he had not been touched intimately for a whole year. "I wanted you so badly, at that moment in your car. When I got to my place I realized how it must have looked, my leaving so fast. I didn't know what to do, how to let you know that it was me and not you."

She had been smoldering since meeting him and now she ignited, fingers entwined in the hair at the base of his skull, relishing in the silky feel of it. His face was hot and his body was electrifying. His desire was evident. She knew at that moment that she would ride the wave to which ever shore it was going to crash on.

Matthew stepped forward guiding her down the hall towards the living area, all the while smothering her with soft kisses.

She pulled his shirt out of his jeans, unbuttoned it with trembling fingers and placed her hands flat on his chest, eyes never leaving his. The feel of his skin against her palms increased the depth of her desire. His heart was racing. Undoing her pyjama top, sliding his hands to her side, he pulled her closer, melting into the softness of her breasts, noting her hard nipples pressing into his chest, all the while trailing kisses down her neck across her shoulder.

She was more beautiful than he had imagined. Her skin glowed under his gaze as they continued their exploration of each other, progressing towards the bedroom. Her lips were swollen and hungry for his. Sliding her tongue in his mouth, he tasted of mint. He took her lead exploring her mouth, gently at first but becoming increasingly more urgent.

Matthew felt as if he had been in a desert forever and now he had just found the most exquisite oasis. It replenished his parched appetite. It revived his soul and continued to melt the ice from his veins. He hadn't realized how cold he had felt, how removed from life he had become. He felt alive for the first time in a long time.

Christina's pushed his jacket and shirt over his shoulders. When they reached the bedroom he looked into her eyes, asking silently, and she responded by pulling him towards the bed and tumbling onto it, oblivious to their surroundings, cocooned in the sheer ecstasy of the moment.

The silence was broken by Christina's moans of pleasure and Matthew's gasps as they both rode the wave to its inevitable conclusion. The exquisite feel of her was almost more than he could handle. His mind was reeling, his body was on fire. Surrounded by her, kissing her continually, her neck, her face, her lips, he revelled in the feel of her curls as he entwined his fingers and stared at her flushed face. He was close to tears as he watched her ride out her orgasm.

Christina came back to earth basking in the afterglow of the near out-of-body experience. No man had ever taken her anywhere near that. If she had any doubts about her decision they had been banished, at least for now.

He smiled. "There you are."

All of a sudden the smile slid from his face. He slipped from her and lay beside her. She felt him distancing himself and now all the warmth had receded. She was troubled by his mood. She reached for him but he moved away slightly.

Christina turned her back to him trying to analyze his strange reaction. After a moment or two he spooned into her, bringing his arm over her ribcage and his leg over her thigh. He buried his face in her hair and inhaled deeply. He whispered, "Are you alright?"

She pressed into him and nodded. He tightened his embrace on her waist.

"Good."

She fell asleep like that, troubled by his momentary recession.

Chapter 9

He woke at dawn. He did not want to disturb her, she looked so peaceful. Lying there, he wondered if he should stay or go. He felt happy, relaxed and ready to do it all again. It seemed he was going to have to learn restraint.

She woke to the smell of coffee as Matthew entered carrying two mugs, wearing only his jeans. She stared at the apparition in front of her, thinking she must still be asleep. Rubbing her eyes, she realized that it wasn't a dream. Oh he was so hot! She almost gasped at the sight of him.

"Hope you don't mind but I went rummaging around your kitchen. He placed her cup on the bedside table. She shuffled up the bed taking the sheet with her.

He looked amused as he moved back to the other side of the bed. Leaning up against the headboard, drinking his coffee, he marvelled at how right this morning felt.

"Run this morning?" he inquired, with a smirk on his lips and a glint in his eye.

"What!" she exclaimed. "I hardly think so. I bet walking might be a challenge today. Why do you think I'm still in bed? I haven't dared try to get up. I think I will be legless and embarrass myself by falling on the floor." They laughed, and she was captivated by those shining green eyes and his inviting lips, to say nothing of his chest that rose and fell displaying his well-defined pecs.

All of a sudden he was off the bed. "Come on." He came round to her side and threw the sheet back, momentarily embarrassing her. Lifting her out of the bed in one swift movement he carried her to the bathroom. He placed her gently on her feet and held onto her body. She kept her arm round his neck for reassurance and her knees collapsed.

"Steady there." He pulled her upright and she said, "Just testing! Fooled ya ha."

"Good thing I'm a chivalrous guy, then." He held her close;

she ran her hands down his arms, relishing in the feel of his taut biceps and muscular forearms. He responded by kissing her still sensitive lips, then let her go. He retreated to the bedroom.

She stood in front of the mirror and stared at herself. *Oh my god, I look like I've just been...* she smiled. She washed up, cleaned her teeth and, putting on her robe that hung on the back of the door, returned to the bedroom to finish her coffee. Matthew had resumed his previous position against the headboard, legs crossed, looking like he had always belonged there.

His face brightened. "Feel OK now, do you?" His hair was mussed up and he had a shadow of stubble... His bare chest set her heart fluttering. She was committed now and she knew it.

She crawled over the bed and kissed him hard on the mouth. "I'm glad you stopped by. Last night was awesome."

He returned her kiss and she felt him smiling. Breaking the kiss, she took his hand and began pulling him off the bed. He followed willingly. Leading him to the bathroom, she closed the door, looked into his eyes and said, "Shower sex?"

Taken by surprise, he gave an involuntary cough. "Don't you have any shame?" he said. He stepped forward and turned on the shower. Turning back to her he moved up close and pulled on the ties to her robe and let it fall open. He drank in her perfection. His belt and jeans were history before the shower was even heated. It was his turn now. He kissed her and ran his hands either side of her ribcage, sliding them to her back, feeling her smooth skin pressed into him. Everywhere his skin touched her, was so hot it burned. His body was hard and his kisses insistent. His eyes, darkening with desire, held her gaze.

He pulled her to him. Things took a much more leisurely pace, both of them delighting in the experience, washing each other with hands covered in jasmine shower gel. She noted every curve on his perfect body, how sculpted his muscles were, his lean torso, his thick, toned forearms and strong, yet gentle hands. When she slid her hands down and reached his left thigh, she felt the scar that ran down towards his knee. "What happened here?" she said, caressing the length of it. He paused for a minute and said, "One day, but not now. It was a long time ago." She continued her slow purposeful exploration of him while his hands slid gently over her shoulders, her breasts; he circled the hard nubs of her nipples with his palms, rolling them between his thumbs and forefingers. Sliding his hands round her, he stepped behind her and saw the small butterfly tattoo on her shoulder blade. He hadn't noticed it before. He kissed it.

"This is beautiful, delicate, yet strong, just like you." He kissed her neck and circled the shell of her ear with delicate strokes of his tongue. She felt his hot urgent breath. Reaching over her head, she buried her fingers in his wet silky hair. Her senses were drenched in him. His arms enveloped her, his palms flat on her stomach drawing her to him. Turning within his embrace she saw the passion and the lust behind his dark, emerald eyes. "Please," she gasped. "Now."

She spent the afternoon indulging herself, remembering every detail of Matthew. Her curiosity was piqued by the discovery of his scar. He was a mystery to her. He emanated self-confidence, but then every once in a while she would notice a frisson of doubt that swept across his face, a hesitation, as if he were thinking better of it.

Except for the interview, she knew next to nothing about him. Her experience of soldiers was non-existent. She already admired his commitment to serve his country. She realized he was brave and principled. What was holding him back?

Returning to his penthouse, Matthew asked himself if he had lost his mind! He was a pretty disciplined guy, or so he thought, but for some reason he seemed to be out of control. A year of celibacy was probably why, or at least that's what he wanted to think. He still felt like he was cheating on Vivienne.

He needed to get some perspective on all of this. He had felt so happy and comfortable this morning, but now he was restless and wound so tight he was pacing his floors.

"Goddammit, I have to get a grip." He kicked the end of his couch then realized that this was not helping anything.

He took a deep breath. Running his hands through his hair while heading to his bathroom, he passed by his dresser, and hesitated...

"Vivienne," he whispered, "you still have such a hold on me, my heart is still broken." Looking at his distraught face in his bathroom mirror, he wondered why Christina would even bother to pursue him? Surely she must realize what a jerk he is. He had been sending her mixed messages and she had sent one very clear one. While shaving he made a decision.

Chapter 10

He took his cowboy hat and his long drover coat from the closet. Grabbing his keys, he left his apartment, slamming the door behind him in his rush to get out.

"Dad, I'm coming over, I want to ride Phantom – is he in the pasture or the barn?"

"Hey son, what's the matter? No *Hi how are you*?"

"Nothing's the matter," he replied sharply. Then calming his voice, he said, "I'd just like to ride Phantom, he needs the exercise."

"OK, I'll bring him in. Are you on your way now?"

"Yes, I'm just leaving town. Thanks, Dad, see you in about an hour. Sorry I was a bit sharp."

Driving into the yard he saw Phantom already tacked up and tied to the veranda rail, waiting patiently.

He was greeted by a loud whinnying and Phantom started shaking his head in anticipation.

Matthew pulled up and greeted Phantom through his open car window."Hey buddy, been waiting long?"

He grabbed his hat and coat, as it was quite cold today, then entered through the front door. "Hi there, where is everyone?"

His mother appeared wearing an apron and drying her hands, anxiously sweeping her gaze over his face."Matthew, hello," she said, proffering her cheek for a kiss. "Is everything all right? Did something happen with one of your clients?"

"No Mum, just some stuff going on, nothing really, I just need some good country air and maybe some home cooking," he said with a grin.

His father appeared, also looking concerned. "Thanks for saddling Phantom up for me, Dad. I'm just going to get my boots." Phantom was eager as Matthew approached. Patting his neck, Matthew mounted him and leaned forward to release the rein from the rail, saying into Phantom's ear, "I need help, buddy; we are going to have to figure this out, just you and me, right?"

Phantom answered with a snort and Matthew turned him towards the back pasture gate.

Once through the gate, he urged Phantom into a smooth and relaxing gallop, just what he needed right now. The biting wind in his face was exhilarating and served to blow away some of the lingering frustration that had caused his outburst.

He and Phantom had formed a trusting and lasting bond. Phantom was no longer the feisty, young, bay-coloured stallion. As Phantom matured, so did their relationship. Matthew knew he could count on him to be sure-footed and brave, having proved that once already, remembering the incident one spring at the river when he and Phantom were nearly swept away by the current. However, Phantom had remained calm under the circumstances and gained the safety of the far bank, all without unseating Matthew.

They kept up a steady pace, the property now a distant speck behind them. His troubled mind eased and he began to analyze the past few weeks.

Christina had come into his life when he thought there was no solution to his despair. He had very nearly given up on himself, resigned that he would never again feel the way he had with Vivienne. He had attempted to compartmentalize his guilt, locking it away in that part of his brain that now seemed so full. It had worked, until last night. Somehow, unexpectedly, in the height of his passion he felt that he should not be enjoying what was happening between them. He was sure he had betrayed Vivienne's love, love that he had treasured beyond anything else. But then he had betrayed her again this morning, hadn't he? How could anything be so good and at the same time feel so bad? He knew that Christina had fallen hard for him. Was she in love with him? He didn't know. He did know that she didn't deserve to be treated badly. Mind you, he had warned her at the restaurant, had noted the relief she displayed upon hearing that he was not married.

He wanted to be loved again. His toughness and his bravery were enhanced by Vivienne's love, wanting her to be proud of him and wanting to protect her from all danger.

Now, he had to make it all relevant again. Perhaps Christina would be the catalyst for that, maybe help to heal him. He hoped so, because he was banking on it. He hated being alone. Paying little attention to where he was headed, he soon found himself far from home. Feeling Phantom's heaving flanks beneath him, Matthew was suddenly brought back to the present. He realized he had run Phantom too hard. "Whoa, Phantom." He pulled him up, gently bringing him to a walk. Within a few minutes Phantom had recovered. He was still hot, sweating, but breathing evenly.

Matthew stopped and dismounted, patting the horse's neck as they walked. He headed towards the trees that bordered the fields and finding a clearing a short way in he dropped the reins and settled on a tree stump. Phantom must have been grateful for the rest, as he snorted and began nibbling at Matthew's arm. Sitting, Matthew stroked Phantom's velvety nose.

Protected by the trees surrounding the clearing Matthew did not notice the wind beginning to blow harder; Phantom did though, and raising his head he sniffed the air and became restless. Matthew looked up. "Come on buddy, time to go."

He mounted and they began their journey home. Soon realizing that this was going to be one hell of a storm, he urged Phantom into a gallop. Once out in the open, controlling Phantom took all of Matthew's skills. Phantom was spooked by the roaring of the wind and the rain that was now sheeting over them. He turned Phantom back towards the edge of the forest, looking for shelter. Phantom reared up, almost dumping Matthew. Struggling to control him, Matthew headed back into the trees. To calm him, he positioned Phantom with his rear to the wind and rain. He stroked the horse's neck and, reassuring, said, "Hey, I won't make you go through this. It's all right, we'll wait it out here, buddy."

It was a fast-moving storm and soon the winds died down and the rain stopped, giving way to clearing skies and bright evening sunshine that was already fading. The air was cool and had a clarity to it that only came after a storm. Matthew felt that the storm had served to bring some clarity to his dilemma as well. He turned Phantom round and they made their way back. Revived, Phantom knew he was headed in the direction of home. Ears pricked and head held high, the setting sun high-lighting his shining coat, he sped across fields soft from the rain, water splashing to his belly and soaking Matthew's boots.

Arriving home, Matthew spent the next hour grooming Phantom. When he finally entered the house, he pulled off his wet boots and walked barefoot into the kitchen, to the aroma of homemade apple pie. His mother watched him approach, relieved that her son seemed to be OK.

"That smells really good, Mum. Is there some for me?" he brushed a kiss over her cheek before seating himself at the end of the breakfast bar."I was a bit worried," she replied, relief evident in her voice. "You were gone a long time and you seemed distracted when you left. You must have been caught in the storm. How was Phantom? I know he hates the wind."

"A bit of a handful but we're back now."

She placed a piece of pie in front of him. Standing opposite, she looked at him for a long time. She knew he was not one to share his worries or his fears. She'd known that ever since he had joined the Special Forces. He was independent and successful; nevertheless, he was still her son.

"Matthew, look at me. Is there anything you want to discuss?"

He paused, fork part way to his mouth. "No, I'll work it out. In fact, I have already. Pie's great by the way."

His mother sighed, likely resigning herself to the fact that he wouldn't tell her, for he had never told her how much pain he was in after Vivienne's death.

Bidding his parents goodbye, he settled in for the drive home. He silently thanked Phantom.

He stopped for take-out. He liked curry but found the preparation was long and tedious, so the perfect solution was the Bombay Star.

Entering his apartment, he hurried to the kitchen and grabbed a fork. He actually felt hungry tonight and ate with gusto directly from the container. Turning on the TV he watched the news and soon learned that the body found under the exit ramp was identified as a member of organized crime, allegedly involved in prostitution and human trafficking. He fleetingly wondered who had killed him.

He showered and was immediately taken back to the morning, smiling, reliving all the wonderful things she had done to him. His leg was aching and he recalled her reaction when she discovered his scar. He stood under the shower head and let the jets play on his body, relieving the aches and pains, realizing he was not that young anymore. Military life had taken a toll.

Stepping out of the shower and towelling himself off he glanced in the mirror and noted that he looked refreshed, unlike the last few weeks where everyone kept asking if he was alright. He put on his favourite pyjama bottoms then checked his phone. There was no message from Christina.

It was getting late. He sent her a text.

Smiling, he placed his phone on the ottoman and channel surfed, waiting.

Chapter 11

Her heart skipped a beat when she heard her Blackberry ping.

Lying in bed, she leaned on the headboard and opened the message. When she read it, her stomach rippled with pleasure.

Christina, showering will never be the same. Can I have a repeat performance please? You aren't the only one weak at the knees.

She replied,

Encores are always welcome.

Relieved, Christina fell asleep with pictures of emerald eyes dancing in her head.

On Monday morning she began to tackle the human trafficking article with renewed vigour. Her attempt at information-gathering had failed miserably. She was still haunted by the death of her informant. Going online had given her a lot of general information but she needed more firsthand knowledge, but where was she going to get that? Mulling it over, she left her computer and decided to make some coffee. Upon her return she still drew a blank. It was early morning, cold and clear, and she decided that a run might help her, if not in mind at least in body. She warmed up with stretches in the parking lot then took off down the street, passing several parked cars including a black sedan.

Its occupants were glad to finally have something to do.

Her favourite music was playing on her iPod and she was soon "in the zone." She didn't see or hear the car following at a distance. Running relaxed her and her mind started to wander back to her last run. She grinned, remembering the surprise on his face when she overtook him going up that hill. She knew that if she wanted to keep up with him, she would have to take her running more seriously.

Returning to her apartment she showered and sat back down at her computer. She still had no resolution to her problem. Her thoughts turned to Matthew; she wondered if he too was having trouble concentrating. She wanted him to call her, she wanted to see him. She wanted to make love to him again. How could she be so needy, having spent her entire adult life being independent. She had never been in love, infatuated maybe, when she was younger. Sex had been, well, just sex.

She picked up her phone.

Matthew was in his office early on Monday. He greeted Anne, who noted that he looked particularly handsome this morning in his black Hugo Boss suit, black shirt and a green tie that highlighted the colour of his eyes. She also noted he seemed to be very happy, something she had not seen for a very long time.

At his desk he powered up his laptop. Vivienne appeared in front of him. He paused for a minute, still not having the courage to change his screen saver.

He turned away and looked out over the city.

His iPhone buzzed insistently. He checked the caller ID, smiled and answered, "Good morning, Christina."

"Hi there, I hope you don't mind the interruption." Her voice trailed off, as if unsure of the reception she was going to get.

"I am delighted to have such a pleasant interruption." While waiting for a reply, he leaned back in his chair and felt a thrill travel through him.

"I have a problem. I hope you can help me with it," she said eventually.

"Of course, does it involve showers or weak knees?" He laughed and she became hot and her breathing erratic.

"Well actually, no."

"Oh." He sounded disappointed.

"Stop! It's bad enough I can't concentrate on anything today. I have a project I'm working on. It involves human trafficking and I wondered if you have any contacts in the police department?"

"I may, what's it worth?" His voice was smooth, sexy and full of humour.

"You never know what I might pay."

"I'll call someone I know and get back to you soon." He took a deep breath... "Christina, can I see you after work? I am having some issues concentrating as well you know."

She was silent for a minute. "Yes, I would really like that."

"I'll come by. By then I might have a contact for you."

Matthew flipped through his phone and found Detective AJ Albert's contact info. They had worked together recently when a prominent visitor from UAE came to town for meetings with oil executives. He had provided personal security.

He made a call and got the message machine.

Human trafficking could be a dangerous thing to get caught up in. Wasn't that a bit risky? He was beginning to think that there was a lot more to Christina than he realized.

AJ called back late in the afternoon.

AJ was reticent. Organized crime was heavily involved in human trafficking and he didn't recommend anyone go down that road. He said he would be willing to meet her to explain.

Now Matthew's concern was justified.

When she opened her door, he handed her flowers then pulled her to him. "I have waited all day to do this." He kissed her hard on the mouth. Responding, feeling his heat and revelling in the smell of him, she leaned into him pushing her fingers into his hair. He ran his tongue over her lips.

He followed her to the kitchen where she put the flowers in a vase and placed them on the dining table. "Thank you," she said, smiling at him. "Wine?"

He nodded and she poured him a glass. She handed it to him, he raised his glass.

How inviting and sexy he looked in his suit and green tie. She came round the island leading the way to the couch. They both sat, no gap between them this time.

Stroking her cheek with his knuckle, he said, "It seemed like a long day today."

She shuddered at his touch. "Yes, but it was worth the wait."

After a few seconds he put his arm around her shoulder pulled her to him and kissed her neck, "Do you like what is happening to us?" he whispered, brushing his lips over her ear.

"I do," she said in a voice she hardly recognized.

"I want to know more about you, you fascinate me. You're confident and poised. Where did that come from?

"I learned at a very young age not to rely on anyone."

"Why?" he asked.

"I don't have anyone reliable in my life. I do all right." She shrugged and tried to make it sound as if it was no big deal.

Matthew's heart faltered slightly. "Where's your family, your Mum and Dad?"

"I don't have any family. Well, none that I could call upon."

"Are they dead?"

"I don't know."

He queried how this beautiful and charismatic woman could be all alone?

No wonder she appeared so fiercely independent!

Matthew waited for her to explain. and realized that she was not going to. He thought of all the had people on his side

– Vivienne, Dan or his Mum and Dad, as well as his sister. Living in the armed forces, he had been trained that everyone has someone they can count on. Someone always had your back. He found it hard to imagine that she was the only one responsible for herself. He was trying to imagine what that was like. After all, where would he have been after Vivienne's death? What a lonely existence hers must be.

"I've been thinking, Christina. I kind of like being with you. I've been on my own for a long time now. I don't like it very much..."

She turned her face away and stayed silent.

"Christina?" he pulled her closer. "Look at me." He placed his hand under her jaw and drew her face to his, her tears threatening to spill. He brushed them away with his thumbs.

"Jesus, don't cry. I didn't mean to upset you. I just need to understand you a bit better, tell me what I have to do to get you to stop?"

He held her pressed to his chest, kissing the top of her head.

She was overwhelmed with his scent and his concern. Her loneliness overwhelmed her sometimes. She had hidden it well, up until now.

Sniffing she spoke into his chest. "I'm sorry, really. People seem to disappear on me. I find it hard to believe that you would want me."

After a pause she said, "Matthew..."

"Yes."

She breathed in a long deep breath.

"Go on," he whispered.

"You wear your heart on your sleeve. I wish I was that open. I wish it was that easy for me, but I learned to hide everything. But then you came along and for some reason I feel I can tell you anything and you will listen, you hear me, you care. No one ever had any concern for my feelings, no one ever cared, not like you do. Who am I? I don't know who I am. I don't know...."

He pushed her upright. He looked her in the eye and said, "I promise to be there, to be reliable. The weekend was amazing. I want more of it. I need it, I need you. I think we can help each other. How about it? I am willing to try."

"You have no idea what you are getting into."

"I'm used to difficult situations." He smirked, raising one eyebrow. "Surely you can't be that hard to deal with?"

He kissed her cheeks, tasting her tears. His hands gently caressed her fears away as she clung to him.

He knew he was committed now and somehow it felt right. He had not quite laid his demons to rest but he was a lot closer to being whole again. He wanted to help her be whole.

Her face was serene and her cheeks flushed. He recalled the evening before, her calling out his name as she surrendered herself to him on the couch. He now slipped out from under her, trying not to wake her. He placed a cushion under her head and went to her bedroom. Bringing her duvet back.

It was late and he had not even told her of his conversation with Detective Albert. She really did look like an angel sleeping there.

Finding his clothes tangled with hers in the mess on the floor, he dressed in the bedroom. Looking around, he noted once again the lack of family photos.

He left closing the door quietly behind him. The cold crisp air sharpened his senses. Walking to his car in the quiet of a predawn morning, he felt exhilarated.

For some reason the skin at the back of his neck started to prickle. He scanned the area, pinning his gaze on a black sedan. He questioned its presence at this time of the day but dismissed it as being extra cautious, a remnant from his deployment days.

By the time he reached home the sun was rising. He put on the coffee pot. Passing by his dresser on the way to his shower he glanced at the empty space. This time he smiled and, like the sunrise outside, he felt a small crack opening up inside him, allowing a shaft of bright sunlight to stream in at last.

The two observers outside Christina's apartment building were not there voluntarily. Their boss was disturbed by the prospect of any exposure about his business.

"It sure is getting cold. How much longer do you think this is going on for?"

"Here, have another sandwich. My coffee's cold! I thought Bryson was going to give us something to go on tonight. All he wanted to do was get her naked. What did Carmine find out about him anyway?"

"He's some kind of security specialist, owns his own company. Jeez I'm fed up with sitting in this car every day."

"Yeah, after the phone call we picked up this morning, I thought we might have something to go on."

"I wonder what he knows and just who he contacted at the police department..."

Despite sleeping on the couch, Christina was rested when she woke, but disappointed that he was not there with her.

She thought how considerate he was, bringing her duvet out and how sincere he sounded and what a great lover he was.

She felt embarrassed that she had broken down that way. It was not in her nature to let anyone see her weakness. Somehow it seemed alright with him. His reaction confirmed her suspicions – he was unique. She had never been able to keep a boyfriend for any extended period. They were always so shallow. Matthew was willing to take a chance on her, even though her upbringing bore no resemblance to his.

She put on the coffee pot. A shaft of sunlight heightened

the vibrant colours of the flowers on her dining room table. She leaned over them, breathing in their scent, filling her with reminders of how he smelt, aftershave and sex. She hugged her naked self, already missing the feel of his strong hands moving over her body, the slightly calloused fingers sparking on her skin wherever they touched.

Her Blackberry pinged, bringing her out of her reverie. Shuffling through her clothes on the floor, she picked it up.

My angel, you are beautiful when you are sleeping.

She grinned and replied:

I'm missing you already. Sorry about crying on your tie :(

"Help me understand this. You two have been sitting on her ever since we silenced Manny, so why in hell don't we have any more information?"

"Bruno, give us a break, we have been freezing our asses off. We bugged her apartment. All we have so far is a detailed account of his lovemaking skills. Interesting I must say, but no mention of anything to do with our business."

"Why would she ask for help from Bryson? When did they meet?"

"As far as we can tell it has only been a few weeks."

"If we keep on her, surely she will have a meeting soon. There must be some sort of a deadline, even if she is freelance."

"Just our luck she has a guy who is in that kind of business, makes it hard to put him under surveillance."

"Well, we have some other business to attend to." Bruno laid out his next business venture. "There's a lot of money at stake here. Make arrangements for a meeting with Carmine over on Dorchester Street or Waterloo, I'll need to see the girls he sends me. I need both of you to escort them to Texas."

"OK boss, but that leaves no one to take care of Miss Nosey Parker."

"You'll only be gone two days. We need to get this done soon."

"I'll get over there now, boss."

Chapter 12

He smiled on the way past Anne's desk, greeting her with more than his usual disarming manner. He was positively floating, or so she thought. She had not seen him this animated for ages. She felt a little jealous of whoever was behind this sudden change. She guessed it was probably that reporter.

"I have a lot to do today," he said, still smiling, on his way to the coffee machine. When he returned he said, "I hope you enjoy today, Anne."

He closed his office door and seated himself at his desk. Opening his laptop, he hesitated for a second before hitting the power button. He waited anxiously while it loaded.

Vivienne was there once more. He stared at her for a long time. His expression hardened. He took a deep breath and right clicked.

His heart rate was slightly elevated and it took a few seconds to return to normal. His finger trembled slightly. Pressing delete was painful.

He whispered, "Love you always."

Leaning back in his chair, hearing the familiar squeak, he remembered the day he had asked her to marry him. He had taken her to the ranch. The ring was burning a hole in his pocket as he practiced his proposal. They sat on a ridge in his SUV watching the sunset over the mountains. She loved sunsets and that day promised a good one.

Just as the sun was about to sink behind the mountain, it shone so brightly it hurt their eyes. It shimmered and then it was gone. Then Venus was there, shining like a diamond in the velvet sky.

They were standing in front of his car, leaning on the hood. What better time than right now. He removed the box from his pocket.

"I have a diamond just like that one up there."

He had opened the box. She was staring between him

and the ring box. He remembered her tears making her eyes shine even brighter in the gathering dusk. She gasped and put her hands to her mouth.

"It would be my greatest wish come true if you would marry me. I need you next to me every day. I feel as if I was born to just love you, to take care of you. I promise I will always be there for you, forever. Please share my life."

He raised his coffee mug and had to make a concerted effort to steady his hand.

Drinking his coffee, looking back at his desktop, he found it strange, staring at the blue background.

Opening his e-mail, he began his usual morning task. He soon found that he had plenty to think about and lots to deal with.

He picked up his phone.

I am having a hard time concentrating again today, when can we get together? Soon I hope.

There was a reply almost immediately.

So am I, but I have work to do, remember.

He answered,

So do I.

He scrolled and hit call.

"That's better," he said when she answered on the first ring. "I like hearing your voice."

"I love to hear you also."

"We never did get to discuss your project did we? Perhaps we could try again soon."

Christina needed no encouragement, "Any time."

"I'll let you know when."

Feeling elated, he called Detective Albert.

"Here we are."

Matthew parked outside a bar that neither of them were

familiar with. This one was owned by a couple of retired cops. It was not that busy. There were a few men sitting at the bar and a couple of the booths were occupied. Matthew saw AJ in a booth and steered Christina toward him.

'Hi, AJ, I'd like you to meet Christina Melville, journalist extraordinaire," he said, grinning at her.

AJ was an intimidating figure, about six feet two, broad shoulders and large hands. His hair was shaved to within about an inch of his head. He looked to be around forty-five. He was wearing a suit and a dress shirt but no tie. It was obvious that he was armed. His expression gave nothing away. He would be quite good looking if he smiled once in a while.

"Good to meet you, please have a seat."

After the waiter brought their drinks he looked at Christina and said, "I'm not sure you should be doing this. These people play hard ball, and we've been trying to nail the ring leaders for some time now."

Matthew had his arm around Christina's waist and his grip tightened slightly.

"Off the record, alright." He gave Christina a warning look" We had an informant within the organization. You heard the news about the body found under the exit ramp a few weeks ago? Well he was under cover. He was a good cop. He had infiltrated the organization about two years ago. No reporting on that though."Christina paled and drew in a deep breath.

AJ looked at her and said, "So you can see how it might be hard for you to get any info. Also, I don't recommend making contact with them. It would be better if they didn't know who you were."

Matthew still had his hand round her waist and felt her reaction. He looked at her quizzically. She chose to ignore him, and instead concentrated on what AJ was saying.

"We know that the boss here in the city is a guy named Bruno Calibri. He has a very impressive house just outside of town. He keeps a girl there and manages at least another ten.

They work Waterloo and Dorchester streets. That seems to be his territory. The money they bring in is astronomical; these girls are virtually sex slaves. We think that the ringleader is actually in Texas." Before parting, AJ gave her the names of some NGO organizations who were trying to help extract these girls.

"Perhaps I should change the focus of my article," she said.

Stepping out into the bright sunlight, Matthew observed the change in her attitude. She seemed anxious and somewhat distant.

"Did you get what you wanted?"

"Yes, yes definitely some good information I can work with." Concern still evident in her expression.

"Thank you for setting that up," she said, leaning over and kissing him on the cheek once again smiling and looking more relaxed.

"You're welcome. Far be it for me to advise you on how to go about your job, but don't you think it is a bit too dangerous to be stirring up that hornet's nest?"

Christina had never been in this position before.

"I have been doing this for a while Matthew, but thanks, I'm sure it will be fine."

He didn't reply.

It was late afternoon when he returned to his office.

"What's up, Matt?" Dan had entered his office almost un-noticed.

"Oh... nothing, Dan; how are things in Sudan?"

"Much better. I think there has been some progress. We need to stay there for a while longer. Ty says things are tense but not violent right now. He says training the employees is not too bad. They are fast learners apparently."

"Good. I hope we can get our guys home for Christmas."

"You seem in a better frame of mind lately. The staff noticed as well. Want to tell me anything?"

Matthew's eyes lit up as he exchanged one of those knowing smiles reserved for your best friends. Dan looked at him with an enquiring smirk. "Who is she?"

Christina needed some clarity.

"I need to see you."

Once Christina had made the decision to see Judy she felt better. Judy was her closest friend, she had to admit that she needed someone once in a while and now was one of those times.

"Thanks for letting me come over."

Judy let her in, and they opened the wine Christina brought.

"What's up Chris? You're not one to talk very much."

Christina hesitated before answering.

"I know. I met someone."

Judy looked at her friend.

"I'm not sure that he even likes me really, he keeps sending these mixed messages. I'm confused."

"Who is he?"

"Remember the guy at the restaurant, Matthew? Well I wasn't entirely honest with you."

She related her interview and subsequent meetings.

"I think I 'm becoming too involved. I have never ever felt like this. Sometimes I can't even breathe."

Judy smiled, "I think you're in love silly!"

"I was afraid of that."

"I'm going to show you off tonight."

Matthew was at her apartment. He was waiting for her to appear from her bedroom. When she came out he caught his breath."You are going to be the most beautiful woman there." He came forward and drew her to him, kissing her gently on the mouth. She inhaled his scent and aftershave and kissed him back.

"Thank you," she whispered.

It was a night she had been looking forward to, ever since he had invited her to the special performance at the theatre in aid of wounded veterans. He looked devastatingly handsome in his tuxedo and bow tie. He put her coat over her shoulders, his green eyes lingering on her. He held her hand and escorted her out, her heart racing again.

They arrived outside the theatre and Matthew proudly helped her out, passing the keys to the valet. He placed her hand through his arm and held her tightly as he led her into the foyer introducing her to the colonel of his old regiment.

Dan and Jane arrived.

Dan gave him that look. Smiling broadly, he waited for Matthew to introduce them.

"Dan, Jane, I would like you to meet Christina Melville."

They shook hands and Jane said, "I am so glad Matthew has a date tonight, it's about time."

Christina smiled at Jane. "It's great to meet you. Matthew says you are one of his oldest and dearest friends."

They found their seats. Matthew held her hand all the way through the concert, as if letting go would break the spell. He was absentmindedly sweeping his thumb over her knuckles, sending shivers down her belly to her very centre. Jane was on the other side and she leaned over, part way through, and said in a low voice. "He thinks he is strong but he really needs some-one to help him be that way again." Christina nodded.

"She is a beautiful girl, Matt."

Dan was in Matthew's office and they were reviewing his proposal.

"I know."

"Jane took to her instantly, by the way. She said she thought the two of you would get on well together."

"I'm glad you both like her because I think I am becoming quite attached to her." His eyes shone. Dan had not seen this side of Matthew for a long time.

"Great. It's nice that you can take her home for Christmas this year."

"I'm not sure about that. I don't know what her plans are yet."

Amused, Dan said, "Judging by what I observed, she will be more than willing to spend it with you."

After Dan left, Matthew thought about that for a while. He hoped so, as he did not want a repeat of last year. He had not left his penthouse for the whole week of Christmas, turning off his phone, living in a sort of haze and registering nothing outside of the fact that he was alone. The only thing he did was drink.

Looking back, he saw how it took his mother to bring him back to life. She visited him virtually every day. At first he wouldn't even let her in, but eventually he relented. She forced him to eat. She took him home and made him attend to Phantom. She admonished him and told him Vivienne would have been so disappointed in him. In the end he pulled himself together, making a promise to his mother that he would find a way to move on.

His work had kept him busy. He had heard of a program in Canada that used horse therapy for soldiers who suffered PTSD after serving in Afghanistan. He wanted to see how it was doing and he thought he might like to help start a similar one here.

Christina was feeling more and more secure these days. She had been waiting for the inevitable to happen, but so far he was still around. She had yet to declare her love, afraid he would run. It took all the self-control she possessed to not tell him.

Matthew played his cards close to his chest. Despite this, she had tried to get him to open up to her. She was still waiting to hear the circumstances of his wife's death. She saw his pain and how much he hurt when he even mentioned her name. What would it have been like to be loved that much?

She still cherished her independence but she did feel that at last she was not alone any more. What he gave her was more than she had ever had before, from anyone. All she wanted now was him to love her, any way he could.

His behaviour – not letting go of her hand, the way he had behaved at the concert, his introductions to all his friends and acquaintances – had caused her to realize he really did care deeply for her. He was proud to have her by his side.

He had made love to her that night. His passion intense, his kisses soft and fluttering over her whole body. Her body had trembled as he entered the most intimate part of her, transporting her to a place that left her breathless and sated. He held her in his embrace for a long time afterwards, whispering to her, telling her that she had saved his him.

Chapter 13

The time preceding Christmas was a busy time for Matthew. He often attended charitable functions, fundraisers mostly; ones Vivienne had been responsible for creating. He made large donations to these organizations in her name. Consequently, he was often called upon to address them.

Christina's wish was granted, at least in the weeks leading up to it, as he had made it clear that he wanted her by his side, the perfect partner for these events, beautiful and captivating. Speaking so easily to everyone and well informed on a variety of subjects, she never appeared to get bored, which amazed Matthew. She was more than happy to oblige him.

She was never far from his thoughts. It was hard for him to concentrate on anything these days. He didn't like the idea of her following the leads for her article, he felt she was treading in dangerous waters and his protective instincts were heightened.

It was snowing gently when Matthew quietly came and stood beside her in front of the floor-to-ceiling window and its spectacular view of the Rocky Mountains. He had banked the log fire that glowed in the stone fireplace. He was dressed in his silk pyjama pants, and Christina loved the way they just hung from his hips. Tomorrow was Christmas Day and she was in heaven.

Matthew had surprised her with first class plane tickets to Vail. The lodge was nestled at the base of the mountain and Christina thought it all looked like a Christmas card. They had been skiing every day. She loved the way he was always by her side, even though she was a good skier.

The lodge had a kitchen and a well-stocked fridge. He had made sure there was champagne, enough for their stay, smoked salmon from Atlantic Canada and Beluga Caviar.

He pulled Christina to him, caressing her back through the pink silk nightdress that he had given her earlier.

"Here, have some caviar, it's delicious." She had never tasted anything so exquisite.

"Happy Christmas, angel," he said, sliding his tongue over her lips, savouring the taste of the caviar. After, he held the champagne flute to her mouth and she sipped from it, feeling the sweet sensation as she swallowed.

"Happy Christmas, it is perfect." She opened her eyes and leaned into him and kissed him gently on the mouth.

Her lips still lingering on his, she said, "I am usually on my own."

Matthew couldn't imagine what that would have been like. His family had always celebrated together and he had revelled in the feeling of love that surrounded him at home. He kissed her again gently.

He led her to a bedroom bathed in soft candlelight. The flickering shadows played over his face illuminating his sparkling green eyes.

Standing in front of the fireplace, he caressed her, causing her to breathe in sharply. She revelled in the feel of his taut hot skin, of the desire that emanated from him. Running her hands over his silky skin, she slid them down his arms and over his forearms. He continued his caresses, all the while kissing her face and neck, gasping as she pulled the string on his pyjamas loose so they floated to the floor. He pushed her nightdress up and pulled her to him; skin on skin, she felt every inch of his desire pressed to her stomach.

She pulled him closer. His breathing was ragged as his hot breath wafted over her neck. Josh Groban was singing 'Hidden Away'. As the lyrics washed over her he picked her up and took her to the bed. Placing her gently on her back, he crawled over her, enveloping her in his arms.

She closed her eyes as he kissed first one, then the other, followed by her nose, capturing her bottom lip and pulling it down. He slid his tongue into her hot sweet mouth. He poured all his passion into the kiss, exhaling slowly, absorbing the warmth of her soft body as he held her. He pressed into her filling her completely as she trembled beneath him, her body slick with sweat.

She kissed his neck, and whispered in his ear "I love you" at the height of her orgasm.

He stilled.

Rising up, he looked at her, searching her face. She held her breath, watching his expression as he captured her mouth, playing his tongue over hers stopping her from saying anything else.

Grinding into her, she felt every inch of him as he found his release. She held on to him fiercely, her nails digging into his back, leaving a trail of pink tracks over his shoulder blades as she arched her body to get even closer to him.

He slid both his arms behind her shoulders pressing her to him, making it hard for her to breathe, but making her feel so secure.

Christina awoke on Christmas morning to Matthew's soft kisses on her forehead and his words of Happy Christmas. She sat up and was surprised to find a stocking brimming with gifts. He watched her, enthralled by her reaction. Her eyes were wide and sparkling and she had a grin that was as big as the Grand Canyon. She squealed excitedly and grabbed him, kissing him feverishly, all the time thanking him profusely.

She opened each gift with care. He had filled her stocking with toiletries and cosmetics in all her favorite brands and scents. At the bottom of the stocking was the smallest gift. A square box tied with a red ribbon, opening it she found a pair of emerald and diamond earrings shaped like stars.

"Matthew this is far too generous a gift from Santa Claus," she said with a wry smile. "Did he have some help on this one?"

He kissed her cheek and said, "Guilty as charged." Leaving the room he returned carrying two champagne flutes containing mimosas, which were cold and the bubbles tickled her nose.

She leant back on the bed and looked at him. Tears welling, she said, "Do you know that I have never had a stocking before, not even when I was a kid? I often wondered what I had done that prevented Santa Claus coming to me."

Matthew looked stunned. "You mean to say no one cared enough to do that for you? How did you ever survive your childhood?"

"I waited for it to be over."

"Well, I will have to make it up to you then, won't I?"

"Thank you," she drew him close and kissed him.

Pulling her off the bed into his arms he said, "Come on."

He cooked eggs and bacon, followed by coffee and Baileys then he took her to the Christmas tree that was set up in the corner.

Underneath was a dazzling array of gifts.

They sat on the floor opening the gifts his mother had delivered when she found out he wasn't coming home for Christmas. At first she was apprehensive, but when he finally told her about Christina, she was pleased for him and insisted that she would like to meet her.

Matthew piled the gifts on her lap. She opened each one with care and excitement as if it was the most precious thing she had ever had. The last one was a robin's-egg-blue slim box. She opened it slowly and was overwhelmed as she took out a beautiful diamond and emerald tennis bracelet. The links were shaped like butterflies. The sun caught the diamonds and emeralds set in each wing of the butterflies that chased each other round the bracelet.

"Oh Matthew, it is beautiful. The emeralds remind me of your eyes." He fastened it on her wrist. "I'm glad you like it. You are beautiful, just like a butterfly. Now you have stars that sparkle in your ears and butterflies floating round your wrist." He lifted her chin and placed a gentle kiss on her mouth.

Handing her gift to him, she said wistfully, "I only have one gift for you." He took it with an expectant look on his face. He opened it and saw the custom made black onyx cuff links, MB entwined on them in gold with a diamond set in the centre-holes of the B. She wondered if he would get the significance of them. She looked at him whispering, "I hope you like them."

"I love them." He leaned over and kissed her softly again. "Thank you."

She pulled him close sliding her fingers through his soft curls, kissing him changing the direction of the pressure she exerted on him, pushing his back onto the floor. Straddling him she ran her hands over his chest, feeling him respond to her.

His face became flushed, his eyes darkened and he gripped her tightly round the waist, holding her firmly against him.

"Matthew, I really do love you."

His reaction did not go unnoticed as she watched his jaw tighten imperceptibly and his brow furrow. Her heart stilled as she waited and then she thought that perhaps it was too soon, that she should have shut up!

He pulled her down and fluttered his tongue along her neck, nipping the skin at her shoulder finding that sensitive spot that gave her shivers all over. He ran his hands over her back circling her butterfly tattoo.

"Give me time, Christina."

"Now, it is time for some fun," he declared as they left the cabin behind them. They spent the afternoon on the snowmobile trails.

Christina was holding on around his waist, his body heat keeping her warm.

They stopped to admire the view and after drinking hot chocolate from a thermos, she insisted on taking over driving the snowmobile. He let her after she pouted and pleaded and kissed him.

He knew there was no arguing with her. His eyes sparkled as he observed how much she was enjoying herself. He would never have guessed she was a novice snowmobiler. Only after they returned did she admit it was her first time. He laughed and said, "I'll have to be careful what I agree to from now on."

They played in the snow. He had held back on taking aim at her but once again she surprised him. She was a good shot with a snowball, hitting her target more often than Matthew would have liked. In the end he had enough of the snow trickling down inside his clothing. He grabbed her and rolled her in the snow making sure she was as covered as he was. She tried in vain to wrestle her way out from underneath him. In the end she thought the only way out was to kiss him to death, so she started kissing him and only then did he stop covering her with snow. When he was kissed into submission, he helped her make a snowman in front of the cabin. After, she dropped to the ground and proceeded to make a snow angel. He watched her smiling face. It was a fitting symbol.

In preparation for Christmas dinner, they had showered and dressed. She looked gorgeous in her black Stella McCartney wool dress. Matthew liked the scooped back that exposed her butterfly tattoo. The black dress complemented her emerald and diamond bracelet perfectly. The earrings enhanced the sparkle that shone in her eyes.

Matthew was wearing his charcoal Armani suit and red

silk tie. His new cuff links looked wonderful in the beautiful French cuffs of his crisp white shirt.

They were driven to the restaurant, where Matthew had reserved a table overlooking Vail village. The view was as exceptional as their dinner and Christina fell more deeply in love with him as he dazzled her with his charm and wit. When he raised his glass to her and smiled, he took her breath away.

Matthew had given Christina a Christmas she would remember. He knew she had fallen hard for him, although he had no idea that she would tell him she loved him.

He felt guilty now, as he was trying to deny that perhaps he loved her as well. He should have read the signs, the way she reacted whenever she was near him. There was no doubt he wanted her in his life. She gave him back something that had been lacking of late, a sort of wholeness and a purpose. She, his guardian angel, had rescued him from self-destruction, but try as he might he could not say those three words yet. This morning had been a revelation to him. His heart had nearly broken when he heard that she'd never had a visit from Santa. He had remembered all the anticipation he had felt as Christmas Eve approached.

Now here he was, sitting across from her, admiring her almond eyes, as the firelight played on her face and illuminated her pupils with a golden glow. He could still feel the sensation of her fingernails on his back. How beautiful she was on the outside. What was hiding on the inside? He vowed he would be there for her whenever she needed him, and he would not disappoint. She had been hurt enough for one lifetime. He had given her his body, but he had held on to his heart; she had given him her heart and her soul. He felt responsible for both of them now.

Christina had taken a leap of faith. She couldn't put the genie back in the bottle now.

So he knew how she felt. His reply had surprised her. Not a word or an indication that perhaps he had strong feelings for her. Of course he did. "Give me time," he had said. She was prepared to wait as long as was necessary. She knew he still carried a torch for Vivienne.

Matthew held her close in the limousine on their way back, savouring the scent of her hair. He reflected on his last Christmas, suddenly feeling embarrassed at the way he had behaved. He had not had any control. He squeezed her to him and kissed her neck, whispering in her ear.

"Thank you for being so bold, I would never have found you otherwise."

She leaned over and kissed him. "I'm glad I found you. I knew you were the one for me the moment I laid eyes on you."

She cuddled closer saying, "Oh and by the way you are spoiling me."

"You need to be. It seems to me that no one did very much for you. I, on the other hand, intend to remedy that as often as I can."

They were settled in front of the fireplace on the floor, leaning on the couch, each with a glass of champagne and both staring into the flames.

Christina placed her head on his shoulder and stroked his hair.

"Can I ask you something? What was Christmas like at your house?"

He caressed her face, pushing her hair behind her ear as he looked deep into her eyes. "My home was filled with love and excitement; Mum and Dad went out of their way at Christmas. The house was decorated. We had a large Christmas tree in the living room and another one on the landing. The house smelled delightful... cinnamon, turkey, apple pie. It was full of family and friends and there were lots of games played and lots of laughter.

"My father breeds quarter horses, so we were taken to the stables on Christmas morning to see the horses. They all had a decoration on their stall and we fed them apples left by 'Santa' in a large sack on a hay bale. My sister always wanted to be the first to feed one." Matthew smiled broadly.

"I didn't know your Dad bred horses. You told me you rode and that you owned a horse. I have never ridden a horse. I am a city girl really. That's why I had never driven a snowmobile before. I learned to ski one year, because I had a boyfriend who liked to ski. I thought he would like that but it didn't work out."

"You are very determined aren't you?" he said. "You just to go ahead and make things happen. I'm amazed you never got a visit from Santa." He looked at her as the light from the fire played across her face.

"I was a foster child. I don't know why I was just given away. I never had a real family. I never knew my mother and I certainly didn't know my father. It seemed that Christmas was just for real families. I was always in the shadow of some other kids. They seemed to just forget me. I felt alone and unloved most of the time."

Matthew's heart missed a beat. He pulled her to him and kissed her cheek. Her eyes were moist and shone in the firelight. If he could have kissed all the hurt away that he saw reflected there, he would have.

He held her there for ages and she caressed his arms slowly, committing to memory every solid plane and edge of his muscles. She traced the length of his fingers, entwining them in hers. She turned his hand over and ran her finger over the slight callouses that had formed on them. "Are these from riding?" she asked.

"Yes, and from my job."

"Do you know? When you hold me like that I feel as if nothing can ever hurt me. I have never had that feeling before. You make me feel so safe. You are the kindest man I have ever met."

"I am not infallible you know..."

A troubled expression flitted across his face and his jaw tightened. Christina leaned over and kissed him, tracing the arch of his brow with her finger, as if to smooth away the trouble.

She held on to him with an iron grip when they were in bed.

Before she fell asleep she whispered, "Hold me close please. I am afraid I will wake up and it will all have been a beautiful dream."

He spooned in to her and pulled her into his arms. He wrapped his leg over her thigh, and her head rested on his arm. Placing his hand on her chest he felt her heartbeat, steady and strong, and marvelled at the life she had carved out for herself. With no resentment towards anyone or so he thought.

His admiration for her had grown when he had heard some of her story. The crack in the door to his heart was open a little wider now and the light was shining a little brighter as well.

He woke first, still in the same position he had fallen asleep in. He tried to remove his arm from under her head, managed to extract himself slowly. Sliding from the bed and trying not to wake her, he shook the numbness from his arm. She stirred and moved into the space he had vacated, a small smile on her face. He wondered what she was dreaming about. God she was beautiful, serene. Her messed up hair fell part way over her face. He pushed it back gently and could not resist stroking her cheek softly.

He left the bedroom and put on the coffee pot.

When Christina came quietly out of the bedroom, he was sitting at the breakfast bar, dressed only in his pyjama bottoms, his back to the room, reading the brochure that was left on the counter. Leaning on the door frame she crossed her arms and stared at his back. His broad shoulders were perfectly proportioned, leading to a narrow waist and delightful backside. She deduced that it was the horseback riding that did that. Rippling with every move, the sun playing on his back only served to enhance the effect. After a while she walked towards him. He heard her coming and turned to face her.

She could not resist stroking his back; he was warm and smooth as silk. She slowly slid her hand downward, sliding her fingers in the waist band of his pyjamas, at the same time kissing him on the mouth. He tasted of mint.

"Good morning. Thank you for keeping your promise last night."

"I hope you slept well," he said.

"Never better."

The coffee pot buzzed, and he poured them each a large steaming mug.

Sitting side by side on the couch in front of a roaring fire, sipping their coffee, he felt content and relaxed.

"This is our last day here, Christina. What would you like to do?"

"It's sad that we have to leave. This is the happiest I have ever been. I am feeling selfish right now. I've gotten used to us being together all the time. I don't like the idea of having to share you with anybody."

Matthew looked at her and sighed, saying, "I know, me neither. So, what shall we do today?" he asked, stroking her hair.

"It's a bit late to go skiing now, there will be too many people on the lifts," she brightened her eyes. "How about we take the snowmobile out again? I can show off my newly acquired skills."

Mathew laughed, saying, "I have to get used to you being in charge some of the time, don't I?"

"Yes, you do, like now!" She playfully pushed him back on the couch and straddled his lap. She kissed him hard on the mouth, forcing her tongue between his lips. Matthew smiled, his eyes registering surprise. He thought she might be a handful on occasions, just as Phantom could be. He didn't want to tame her, in fact he loved her aggressiveness. Although sometimes he feared for her safety because he knew she did not always weigh all the options.

The weather was perfect, bright and sunny. The snow was brilliant and blindingly white, sparkling at every turn. She was becoming more proficient in her driving skills and Matthew was happy to sit behind her, pressed up against her, though he did have to warn her slow down on more than one occasion after narrowly missing a tree or two.

They stopped for lunch at the crest of a hill. Sitting astride the snowmobile, facing each other as they ate.

When they had eaten, admired the view and taken a few photos, Matthew said he wanted to take over the driving for a while. Christina pouted for a minute, then kissed him and said she would '*let him.*'

She climbed on behind him and they headed home.

On the way down the mountainside, she became aware of a loud rumbling noise. It sounded like a freight train, but there were no railway lines close by. Christina turned to look and quickly realized what was happening, that this was the noise an avalanche makes. It was pursuing them down the hill sweeping everything in its path aside. "Avalanche!" she screamed at Matthew. He turned and increased his speed.

"Hang on tight!" She buried her head in his back. He managed to keep ahead of the avalanche but he knew it was going to catch them soon. All he could do was pray that it would stop before that happened, but it overtook them where the grade wasn't as steep. It slammed into and over them, bringing the snowmobile to a stop. Fortunately, this was the end of the leading edge of it.

The force of the impact threw Christina off and to the side. The snowmobile stalled as the key was ripped from the ignition and Matthew was lifted and thrown away from the machine, knocking the wind out of him as he landed awkwardly on his left side. He lay there trying to regain his breath, suddenly realizing he had not seen or heard Christina. Panic set in. Yelling her name, he scanned the area close to him. He turned his attention to the snowmobile. The machine was half buried. The snow was piled quite high. Something blue peeking out of the snow caught his eye. He scrambled over and started digging desperately with his hands, trying to determine which way she was lying. He kept digging until he could see that she was lying face down. He dug furiously, getting deeper and deeper. The snow was packed down hard, his hands hurt, his back ached and he was feeling more desperate with every minute that passed.

No, this can't be happening!

Eventually he was able to stand on the snow and reach into the hole. Shoving his hand as hard as he could down and around her body, he pried her halfway up. Now he had her backside and half of her back exposed. She was still buried at her head and her feet.

He started digging above her shoulder. At last he was able to expose part of her face but not enough to expose her nose. He scraped snow from around her chin and her mouth. He could not tell if she was breathing. He grabbed her helmet and pulled hard. Her head came part way up and he was able to get his hand underneath the other side of her head and with all his strength pulled her up out of the snow. Her body was now twisted to one side and her legs and feet were trapped.

He still wasn't sure if she was breathing. He couldn't start mouth to mouth in that position so he dug some more, finally freeing her legs. Kneeling down next to her he fumbled with the strap of her helmet; his fingers were numb and he was trembling all over and his heart racing. He removed her helmet. With trembling fingers, he undid her zipper so that he could reach inside. Pulling her jacket open he checked the pulse in her neck; it was there, albeit weak. Her nose and throat were clear, but she was not breathing and she was white as the snow. Still out of breath he took a large gulp of air and tilted her head back and began mouth to mouth, checking her pulse then waiting a second or two to see if she started breathing. He was having trouble getting enough air into his own lungs. He persisted. Suddenly she took a deep breath and writhed on the snow. Matthew sat back, lifting her head onto his lap. He looked at her and watched the colour began to seep back into her face.

She opened her eyes slowly. He came into focus and she was staring into his concerned face. He smiled with relief, pressing her head to his chest.

"How do you feel, are you hurting anywhere?"

Taking inventory of her limbs, she concluded that nothing was hurting too badly, although her shoulder seemed to be aching. When she began to move it there was a sharp pain that made her wince and cry out.

Matthew immediately stilled her movement. "What hurts? Is it your arm?"

"N-no," she stuttered as the pain subsided, "it's my shoulder."

"Where, at the back or the front?"

"On the top, here." She indicated her collar bone.

"Can you get up? Here, let me help you."

Matthew pushed her upright and then stood, helping her to her feet. She swayed slightly and he steadied her. She was able to stand on her own. Holding her shoulder, she looked at him and said, "How about you? Are you OK?"

"I'm fine, just got the wind knocked out of me, that's all. I'm OK now that I've got you out."

He helped her to the snowmobile. It was partially buried at the back but there was room for her to sit near the front.

"Let me see that." He gently moved her jacket off her shoulder and was relieved to see there was no bleeding.

"Here, put your arm inside your jacket and I'll zip it up as far as I can – that'll help to support your shoulder. Sorry, we don't have anything else to use."

She did as he suggested, and it felt more tolerable.

Matthew stepped back, assessing their situation. He needed to get her to the hospital. Would the snowmobile start once he freed it from the snow? If he called for alpine rescue it would probably take much longer.

He pressed the start button. The engine sputtered and he thought it might catch but it died after a couple of seconds. Well, at least there was life. He left it for a few minutes and decided to remove more of the snow.

Once freed, he dragged it back on the trail.

"OK, Christina, this is how we are going to do this. You can sit in front of me, and I will drive from behind you. It won't be very comfortable for either of us, but it will do the trick."

Once again, he pressed the start button praying it would catch this time. It did, and he was never so relieved as at that moment. Engaging the throttle, they headed slowly down the mountain.

At the Medical Center, after an x-ray, they told Christina that yes, her collar bone was broken, but that there really was no treatment for it other than keeping it in a sling until it healed. She was given pain killers and told to take them every four hours.

Back in the cabin, removing her sweater was challenging, to say nothing of painful, and he winced as she cried out a couple of times. He settled her on the couch and made dinner. He thought she looked very nice in his shirt, that fit more easily over her arm.

Matthew attended to her every need. When he brought her dinner over, she kissed him, running her hand through his soft curly hair. "Thank you for looking after me. I'm not used to all this attention."

He helped her to bed, caressing her arm and her naked body as she lay on her back.

He lay there, staring at the ceiling. Something had shifted between them since the accident.

You love her you know.

He didn't know where that had come from and dismissed it.

He moved away from her so that he was not touching her at all. She moved closer in her sleep, her body missing the warmth and the feeling of security. He gave in and placed his hand under her head, wrapping his arm round her shoulder falling into a troubled sleep.

Chapter 14

The journey home was uncomfortable for Christina but Matthew made sure that she was taken care of. He gave her the pain killers before leaving Vail, which helped, as did being in first class, as she had plenty of room. Sitting next to him, she leant on his shoulder.

Hours later, when they reached her apartment, Matthew told her he would stay with her for the rest of the week. Her heart sang upon hearing that.

"Oh Matthew, you don't have to do that," she said. "I can look after myself. I've been doing it for a long time. Like I said in Vail, you are spoiling me and pretty soon I will be one of those helpless, dependant women."

"Christina," he laughed, "that will never happen to you. You have been independent far too long to change that much in such a short time. Besides I will be able to spend more time with you."

Once back in his apartment he sat for a while before collecting his things. He had considered bringing her here but the thought of taking her to the bed he had shared with Vivienne still didn't feel right. So this had seemed like the best solution. He cared too much for her to just abandon her. Besides, what would his mother have said?

Thinking of his mother, he wondered where Christina's was. She had shut down completely when he had asked about her family. That part of her seemed unreachable. He wanted to ask her, it seemed so juxtaposed to his idyllic upbringing.

When he arrived back at her apartment she had changed her clothes, she now wore a comfortable pair of sweat pants and was wearing her sling outside her zippered matching top.

He kissed her chastely on the mouth and said, "How are

you feeling now? I see you managed to change clothes without me."

"I managed, yes. It hurts quite a bit though when I move my arm any higher than my waist. I hope it doesn't last too long like this. I have to get that article sent."

"Did you consider what AJ said? I know it's none of my business but it sounds dangerous, don't you think?"

Christina sat on the couch and was silent for a few minutes, weighing her answer carefully.

"I have committed to this article, Matthew. I can't just abandon it. My publisher is expecting it soon. I know you feel that I need protection and I love that you do. But please don't fret over me. I'll be fine. Besides, I can look after myself. I've been doing it for years."

She leaned over to him and kissed his cheek.

"I probably am overstepping my boundaries," he replied, looking away from her.

Christina had never lived with anyone and she found the experience a little disconcerting on occasion. She loved the fact that Matthew was there all the time to reach out or touch him anytime. She could bounce ideas off him.

Having someone to rely on made her feel like maybe she was relinquishing some of her fierce independence. She knew she had to learn to strike a balance.

They discussed her article often and she knew he would be upset if she told him about the incident under the off ramp, so for now she had not mentioned it. She valued Matthew's input and respected his opinion.

After all, he knew a lot more about dangerous situations

than she did.

She lay in bed caressing the scar on his thigh one night.

"How did this happen?" she asked.

"I was in Afghanistan on one of my deployments. We were meeting with the village elders. We did a lot of that, hoping to gain their trust and let them know we really were there to try to help them. I was at one of those meetings when a young boy came over to us as we were seated in a circle under a tree with four of the villagers. There were several people milling around us and we were a bit nervous, as there was a lot of tension that day. We felt sure there was something at play there, but we couldn't put our finger on it. We always laid our guns down beside us when we were negotiating. All of a sudden we were attacked by this boy and two of his friends. They rushed us and started stabbing us. One of them killed my friend Brad; he was sitting next to me and I was reaching for my gun when one of them plunged a knife in me."

Matthew paused, his brow creasing slightly. "It was hard to shoot at these boys. We found out afterwards that the Taliban was in the village that day and had promised to pay them if they killed us."

"I'm glad you don't go to those places anymore. Not sure how I would handle that." She kissed his scar and then she kissed him.

He remembered how Vivienne had reacted every time he had to leave. He held Christina a little tighter and returned her kiss.

Chapter 15

"Christina, please you can't go there. Do you know how dangerous it can be?" Matthew was pleading with her. "I've changed my mind. I know I said I wouldn't interfere with your decisions but now that you have decided to go..."

Christina interrupted him.

"Matthew this is my job. This is my life; *this* is what I do. I need to go to find out how human trafficking works down there. Besides, Mexico isn't that far. The trouble there is related more to drugs than anything else."

She was frustrated; Matthew wasn't listening. Ever since Christmas he had been overprotective.

This kind of reaction was not new to her. It usually ended badly and she feared that would happen again.

"Matthew, I'm sorry. I'm going this week." She managed to keep her voice steady and her tears from flowing.

She hung up.

He stared at the phone. His heart was racing. He had already overstepped his mark.

Rising from his office chair, causing it to protest loudly, he left, brushing past Anne, taking her by surprise. All eyes were on him as he hurried through the office door without looking back.

Riding the elevator down to the parking garage, he punched the wall and exited on the run, making a fist of his sore hand as he approached his car.

He peeled out of the garage, cutting off a car as he exited onto the busy street. His heart was still pounding and his body shaking. He had not felt this out of control in a long time.

He was a mess and he was not sure what to do. He was brought back to reality when he nearly rear-ended a car at the light.

The horns blaring in the noon-hour traffic made him realize that he had to calm down. He inhaled deeply while waiting for the light to change.

Without thinking, he found himself on I-84, heading west.

He checked the house and the garage but his parents weren't home. He found his boots under the bench; he was still wearing his suit but disregarded that. Removing his tie and his jacket, replacing it with his father's barn jacket and borrowing his father's cowboy hat as well, he went in search of Phantom. He was relieved to find him in the barn this time.

Phantom whinnied a greeting and Matthew's heart rate and breathing immediately began to slow. He saddled and bridled Phantom, his mind whirling with thoughts of Christina heading into god knows what kind of dangerous situation. Damn she was a handful!

Mounting Phantom in the yard, he set out once again through the back pasture. He urged Phantom into a gallop, and as soon as Matthew felt the wind on his face he felt the anger subside. He concentrated on his riding. His mind began to clear. When he reached the back quarter of the property he sought out the trail that led to the stream. When he reached the river bank he dismounted, allowing Phantom to drink while he sat on his favourite stump for a while, just staring at the river rushing by.

How in hell did I get into this situation?

This time he was not sure what to do. He had been able to make a decision before. Was he using Christina?

This was not him, why had he become so involved? He had to admit that he liked the way she made him feel but he was not ready to admit that he loved her. Hell he was a mess of indecision!

Whistling for Phantom, who had wandered off in search of more appetizing grass, he rose from the tree stump. Phantom returned at a leisurely pace and Matthew remounted him. He was not prepared to return just yet, so he urged Phantom across the river with no particular destination in mind.

Taking it easy, allowing Phantom to set the pace, he recalled when he had purchased Phantom as a yearling at the annual spring auction. Phantom had stood out, not only for his striking appearance, but his feisty attitude. He was one of the largest yearlings there. Being a colt, Matthew knew he would be a challenge to train. He welcomed that challenge and even though he had paid more than he felt he should have, he never regretted that expenditure. Phantom had returned it with his unfailing devotion.

Vivienne had been impressed by Phantom's gentleness, even though she found his size intimidating. She had no experience with horses at all. Matthew had hoped that she would take a liking to Phantom and horseback riding in general. That had not happened, but he was content to leave it at that. It didn't matter there were many other things they did together.

He recalled meeting Vivienne at Dan's house. He had been invited for a barbeque and she was living next door. He had fallen in love the moment he saw her. She was tanned and blond with long legs that wouldn't quit and a beautiful smile. They had hit it off right from the start, spending the day talking and not taking much notice of anyone else. She explained that she worked for a charity that operated in Africa, told him of her ambition to feed as many hungry children as she could.

Life had been good for the two of them. She understood what it was that drove him to be who he was.

Matthew rode along engrossed in his memories and the familiar warmth he felt every time he remembered Vivienne. It was late by the time he returned Phantom to the barn. He groomed and fed him.

No one was home by the time he left. He called his father

from his car, but his father's phone was turned off. They must be at the theatre or a movie, he thought, so he left a message.

When he reached his building he wasn't prepared to go directly to his apartment just yet so he walked to his favourite bar.

Placing a scotch in front of him, Harry said, "Well, I haven't seen you around her for a while, how are you?"

"I don't know, to tell you the truth. Thanks," he said, raising his glass.

Matthew sipped his scotch slowly, letting the warmth envelop him. He stared at himself in the mirror. His mind started whirling again, so he had another scotch. He stayed at the bar long enough to feel slightly buzzed, then walked back to his apartment, realizing that perhaps he should have left sooner. *The hell with it, what do I have to lose now?*

He poured another drink and sat on his couch in front of the fireplace and drank some more until he felt comfortably numb.

Waking up fighting with his bedding, he surfaced from his now familiar nightmare and lay there waiting for his heart rate to subside. With his head full of Christina and Vivienne, he was unable to return to sleep.

He regretted his decision to go to the bar. Falling back into his old habits would not help him.

It was still the middle of the night when he dressed for a run.

The air was cold and the ground was frosty, as he started out for the park, setting a steady pace, noting how beautiful the night really was. He decided to run until he had eliminated all thoughts of Christina and Vivienne.

At one point forced to sidestep a raccoon that scurried across his path, he ran hard, passing the lean-to he had taken shelter in with Christina.

He ran in the silence of the clear moonlit night.

His head was hurting now, and his leg began to throb. He pushed on. Eventually he had to stop. Bending forward, placing his hands on his knees, he tried to catch his breath. He was sweating profusely and he hurt everywhere.

Recovering, he started for home. By the time he arrived his mind was clear but his body was crying out for him to stop abusing it. He stepped into the shower and spent a long time allowing the jets to play over him. He left the shower feeling relaxed, his body still humming with aches.

He dressed for the office in his usual fastidious manner.

He sat at his breakfast bar, drinking his coffee as night receded and the pale light of dawn penetrated his home.

He was there before Anne for once.

He powered up his laptop and immediately regretted removing Vivienne's photo.

Matthew threw himself into his new project.

He looked up when the lights in the outer office came on and watched Anne make her way to her desk.

"Good morning, Anne; now I know how early I have to be to get here before you."

"Oh, you're here already. Hope everything's alright; you left in kind of a hurry yesterday."

"Yes, needed to get away for a while"

Shortly after, Dan, looking concerned entered Matthew's office. He closed the door behind him. "Something wrong, Dan?"

"You were a little distraught yesterday, when you left, and I've seen that look before. Are you OK?"

His chair gave the usual protest as Matthew leaned back.

"Nothing you can help me with. Got some news I would

rather not have heard, that's all."

"Are you sure? I thought things were getting better with you these days. Am I right?"

"Oh God, Dan, I don't know. She is exasperating. Perhaps it wasn't a good idea."

"Of course it is; you have been in a much better place lately." His tone was jovial.

"Have I? I'm not sure anymore, I am so damn confused."

"Maybe you need to cool things for a while."

"Well that won't be hard. We had a disagreement... well, on reflection, perhaps it was a fight. I don't know! I won't be seeing her for a while anyway."

Dan looked dismayed, "Why? What happened?"

Matthew said, reluctantly, "She's going away for research, to Mexico, of all places, but I told her she should stay here. It's dangerous in Mexico."

"Old habits die hard hey?"

"I know. So how do I deal with this now?"

"Can't answer that. Be careful though. I know you. You don't want to end up like last year."

"I'll take that under advisement."

Matt's research led him to a contact in Ontario, Canada. He decided that a trip would not be a bad idea. he instructed Anne to make arrangements – he needed to see how the PTSD program was working.

His trip was planned for the following Monday. Squeezing it in before the opening of the art exhibition at the gallery he had promised the artist he would attend.

He only had to get through the weekend and then he would be busy enough to get back on track. At least he thought he would.

It took a monumental effort for him not to go to see Harry

on Friday night. He had been frequenting the bar far too often, finding solace in the bottom of a glass of scotch. Instead he went home and immersed himself in his research about the PTSD program.

Sleep evaded Matthew once again. His head was pounding, and he wondered what Christina was up to.

Unbeknownst to him she had been Ciudad Juárez for the past week.

It was a hot and humid evening when she had arrived in the border town. She lay in bed glad of the air conditioning in her room.

What had happened?

It was with a heavy heart that she had embarked on her journey. She kept checking for a text or call.

She had been hopeful this time, taking the leap of faith when he asked her to spend Christmas with him. Surely she could combine independence and a relationship? Especially this one! The trouble was it had never worked for her before. She wasn't sure she wanted to go down that road again. Not yet anyway. Every time she thought of him, tears welled up.

No stranger to disappointment, she employed her age-old tactic to deal with it. Immersing herself in her project. This time, however, she was not having any success.

The next day Christina sought out a journalist from the local paper.

She received a warm reception and soon was given the name of a non-profit agency, located near the border that existed for the sole purpose of helping anyone who was seeking a way out of the country. She spent the next few days developing some contacts and decided to extend her visit two weeks.

She was shocked at how easy it was for men to cross the border in search of a prostitute. Everything was so cheap and regulations were lax.

In light of this information, Christina hoped someone would turn up seeking help. It took a few days, but she had just arrived at the agency one day, when a twenty-something girl came in seeking help, having been directed there by the border guards.

The condition of this poor girl appalled Christina. She was starving and it was evident that she had been mistreated.

Feeling sorry for the girl she introduced herself and offered her a can of coke. The girl took it and drank deeply. After finding out her name was Rose she started to inquire about her circumstances.

Chapter 16

"My name's Christina I'm doing research on human trafficking."

Rose stepped back wide eyed. She hurriedly put down the can. "I better be going now." She started for the door but before she got it open Christina grabbed her arm, pleading with her to wait. Rose started to pull herself free. Christina tightened her grip.

"LET GO OF ME!"

Christina immediately released her hold and Rose ran outside and continued running down the dirt road followed by Christina.

"Rose, please, wait up."

Rose dodged down an alleyway.

It was hot and humid and Christina was sweating profusely. But Rose was no match for her speed and almost collapsed on the dirt road. She steadied herself on the wall and Christina stopped in front of her.

Rose started crying and swiped the tears from her cheeks.

"Come back, please "

Rose, eyes brimming with tears, gulped in lungfuls of the hot humid air.

"Why should I? I didn't come here to get caught. I just needed some help. I heard I can get some here to go back to the States."

"Yes they can help you here."

"I really need help. I can't do this anymore. I want to go back. I think it will be safe now."

"Safe now? What do you mean?"

Rose refused to answer and it took Christina's considerable powers of persuasion to calm Rose and convince her that nothing bad would happen if she would only return to the office. Once back inside Rose looked furtively around. She leaned in and whispered, "It was dangerous for me to go back before."

"What do you mean before. Before what?" Once again Rose clammed up.

Christina asked if there was a room she could use.

She settled Rose down on the couch in the only room with a door.

Taking the chair opposite, she said, "What did you mean back there. Before what?"

Rose looked at her for a long moment. "You look kind, but you're a journalist. I don't think I can trust you."

"You can, Rose. I wouldn't be able to my job properly if I didn't gain the trust of the people I write about. I want to help you, all of you."

"What do you mean all of us?"

"Girls like you. Girls who have for some reason turned to prostitution."

"How do you know that's what I am?"

"You came here looking for help. You are certainly in need of it. I can tell. The word is out that this place can help you get out of your situation, otherwise you wouldn't be here. Right?"

Rose sat silently. Christina waited.

Finally, after a deep breath, Rose said,

"Before my father died."

Christina was puzzled.

"Before your father died?"

"Yes."

"Why."

Rose shifted in her chair, anxiously looking around the room.

"Can I trust you?"

"Yes of course, I don't use anything that identifies anyone. No names."

Rose seemed to relax.

"My father sold me."

"Your father *sold* you!"

"Yes."

"What do you mean he sold you?"

"He had gambling debts he couldn't pay. He owed Bruno, my pimp, lots of money. He offered me as payment. I was fifteen. I had no idea what was going on. He took me to Bruno's house one day and said this was where I was going to live from now on. It was a nice house, a great big house. At first I thought I was supposed to be the maid or something but then after a couple of days of not doing anything much except sitting by the pool and listening to a lot of comings and goings I started to get curious. I watched as girls came and went and the phone rang constantly. And then a girl named Starr appeared and she got to stay as well. She was a lot older than me. I asked her what happens in this house and she looked at me incredulously and said, 'You poor naive thing, Don't you know?'

"'Know what?' I said.

"'He'll tell you soon.'

"He did.

"He had me dress up real nice and brought me to the door one day. A limo was there and the driver took me out to a strange place I'd never been.

"It turned out I was to go and see this man. I did and he raped me, he hurt me so bad. Said I was nice fresh meat untouched, he liked that.

"Next time Bruno asked me to get dressed nice, I refused. He took my curling iron that was heating on my dresser and held me down as he stuck it on the inside of my thigh. See here."

She lifted her skirt and Christina gasped as she revealed an ugly scar. Rose was crying now and Christina wanted to stop her but she needed to find out how Rose had ended up in Mexico.

"He sent me out anyway. A different place this time. This man didn't seem to care either, that he was hurting me.

"Not long after that he had me pack my things and told me I was going to Mexico. A vacation, I thought, that can't be so bad. It turns out I recognized a couple of the johns, prominent citizens, and I happen to mention it to Starr. Next thing I know

I'm on my way here with three other girls. I've been here for two years now. They give you heroin and cocaine for free. Keeps us happy. So, can you get me out of here now, today, because if they find out I'm missing there will be hell to pay. At least they can't come after my father."

Close to tears, Christina left the room. Returning a few minutes later she told Rose, "All set, they will look after you now. Thank you. I will do my best to see this is printed and hope it helps to make a difference."

She hugged Rose's frail body and wished her luck.

On the plane home she was still reliving her interview with Rose while formulating her approach to the article she would write.

Upon reaching her apartment her melancholy returned as she wondered what Matthew had been doing in her absence. God she missed him. She picked up her mail and read the newspaper online before resigning herself to a lonely evening in front of the TV.

Canada was cold at this time of year. He was met with an icy blast as he picked up his rental car and drove to the Trump International.

Having investigated the mini bar and not finding any scotch, he left his room and went to the bar and was surprised to find it well stocked with single malts. He ordered a Laphroaig and sat there brooding. He was relieved that the next three days would be busy.

Following the directions from his GPS he drove to the large military base in Trenton. After going through security he was directed to the officer in charge of the program who explained over a cup of coffee how the program worked. They were driven to the stables nearby where he watched the veterans interacting with the horses. He met a number of the veterans and heard how they had been helped by their interaction. How they felt they were not being judged. To a man they all believed that if it had not been for the bonding with these animals their various ailments associated with PTSD would have been more severe.

In fact, this was not a new concept to him. After all, wasn't this what he did whenever he felt the need for solace or to work out his anxieties?

Chapter 17

At the opening of an art exhibit, she allowed the buzz of conversation from the full gallery to wash over her. She hoped this distraction would help her. In the shadows, leaning on a pillar with a glass of wine in hand, she surveyed the gathering of dignitaries. Noting the mayor and councillors, with their partners close by, as well as other patrons viewing the artist's work, her gaze fell on a tall man who had his back to her as he was engaged in conversation with the mayor's wife.

Her heart skipped a beat.

As if he felt her presence, he turned and scanned the crowd. She held her breath, hardly believing her eyes as she stared at the handsome face with the emerald eyes. Her heart stuttered almost to a halt and she felt dizzy. Leaning on the pillar for support, she swallowed a large gulp of the not-so-good wine.

He stared in her direction and then, as if someone snapped on a switch, he was striding through the crowd sweeping surprised patrons aside like Moses parting the Red Sea. His target was in his sights and there was nothing that was going to stop him from gaining it. He side-stepped a surprised waiter (who somehow managed to save the tray full of wine glasses supported on his shoulder) leaving a murmuring crowd behind.

He stopped in front of her, unclenching his jaw and his fists. Breathing heavily, he bent down whispering, "Oh Christina, what happened? I know it's only been barely three weeks but it feels like three years. Nothing is right. Nothing makes sense at all." He grabbed her arms.

Tears started to form and her vision began to blur. His eyes were glistening as well.

After a lingering moment he stepped back, lashes still holding the remnants of his tears. Brushing her thumbs over his closed eyes, he inhaled deeply, holding on to her even tighter.

"We have to leave. I can't wait any longer. I need you to come with me, now, back to my place," he whispered.

He led her back through the crowded gallery, then guided her to elevator, pushing the button impatiently.

The elevator arrived and he pulled her inside, pushing her arms up holding them tightly against the elevator wall, kissing her, his tongue pushing between dry lips moistening them.

As the doors opened he grabbed her hand, pulling her after him so that she had to run to keep up.

Inside his apartment, he urged her towards the bedroom. "Come with me, please Christina. I'm sorry I behaved like that but I have been sick over your whereabouts." Kicking the door closed, he started kissing her again.

Christina shoved his jacket back over his shoulders and yanked his tie loose, pulling it over his head. With trembling fingers, they undressed each other. He dropped his jacket to the floor and reached for the zipper on her dress.

His shirt open, she placed her hands flat on his chest and she felt his hot skin beneath her palms. The was a sharp intake of breath from Matthew.

Pulling Christina close to him he whispered, "I missed this, the feel of your body touching mine everywhere." He walked her backwards towards his bed and gently pushed her down, all the time kissing her eyes, her nose, her forehead. Breathing deeply, trying to steady his progress, he entered her slowly. Now he felt whole again. He lay over her, kissing her passionately and feeling her breathing becoming shallow and fast. She ran her trembling hands over his shoulders and down his spine to the small of his back, squeezing his butt, digging her fingernails in sharply as she pulled him further into her. He exhaled at the sudden pain she'd inflicted and responded, kissing her during a moan of pleasure as he moved slowly inside her, whispering in her ear, "Thank you, my angel, for coming back. I am in need of rescue. I missed you so much. I can't be alone anymore."

This time the wave was more like a tsunami. When it receded, the intensity of their release left them both exhausted but sated. She kissed his chest, inhaling his intense scent. He withdrew from her and settled beside her.

When her euphoria faded, she started tracing the edge of his ear with her tongue and whispering, "I'm sorry. I'm sorry we couldn't agree." She continued, "I had to go. I hoped that you would understand."

Anxiety etched on his face and in his voice. "I don't ever want to feel like that again. Please promise me."

"It's hard for me. You know that right? We'll have to come to some kind of compromise won't we?"

He looked over to his dresser and stared at the empty space.

He didn't feel guilty at all, he felt happy. He made a promise to himself not to fall back into his bad habits again. She did not deserve that.

Turning back to Christina he pulled her to him and kissed her. She wrapped her legs around him and she kissed his chest and caressed his back. She felt him respond with a satisfied groan as he rolled her under him.

She inhaled deeply.

Moving down her body, he trailed his tongue all the way to her navel, circling it slowly and making her abdomen quiver with anticipation. She continued to caress his back, revelling in the silken feel of his rippling muscles as he slid lower and lower, then running her fingers through his damp curls that tickled her inner thighs. He continued his journey down her body.

Christina closed her eyes and succumbed to his exploration.

Chapter 18

Christina was feeling more secure since the gallery opening. They had come to a better understanding. When it came to her work decisions Matthew had agreed to back off as far as he could.

She was working on her article for *In the Know Magazine* every day now, as the deadline was approaching fast. Texting and phone calls were their main source of communication as they'd agreed to stay apart, difficult as it was, while she pushed to finish the article. Even when they talked on the phone, they made sure to talk only about work.

It wasn't easy.

Christina was slowly catching up on her article. Just as she had predicted, she had fallen behind on her timeline. But she was even more determined to get this done. She was sure Matthew would appreciate it as well. The texts became more frequent and more explicit. Matthew had become somewhat of an expert in the communication field and Christina was happy to reciprocate.

She was finally nearing the end. She had been able to describe human trafficking in what she thought was a clear and concise way. She had not named anyone but she made sure there were a few veiled clues, including implicating her city as having one of these active organizations.

Matthew had had no idea how prevalent this particular activity was. He hadn't come in contact with these sorts of criminals. His clients were mostly politically motivated.

Her article would be featured next month. Her editor's queries had come mostly by email but he had called her this last time, impatient to get the article.

Another week.

Matthew was ready for that too, checking the days off his calendar.

Chapter 19

Christina wearing ear buds listening to The Killers, was sitting on her bed working on her laptop when she thought she heard someone entering.

She had relented and given Matthew the access code to the main door and a key to her apartment. He had convinced her that he would not arrive unannounced.

Pulling the ear buds out, she looked expectantly towards the bedroom door waiting for him to call out her name. Nothing. Her adrenalin began to rush through her veins as she heard the unmistakable sound of a gun being cocked, saw movement in her living room and a shadow pass by her partially open door. Suppressing a scream, she held her breath.

Where was her gun? Where had she put it? It was on the other side of the bed in the drawer to her bedside table. Jesus how was she going to get to it now?

While leaning over to that side of the bed her door was violently pushed open. A man holding a revolver aimed it at her. He made a grab for her laptop but she was quicker. He was at a disadvantage, only having one free hand.

Holding the laptop in both hands, pulling with all the strength she could muster, she finally freed it from his grip but then fell backwards off the side of the bed and hit the floor hard. She scrambled to get under the bed just as he came round it. He grabbed her ankle, pulling her out. The laptop had skidded under the bed.

"Get up," he yelled, pulling her by the arm now. His fierce grip caused her to cry out in pain.

"You Melville?" he demanded with a slight accent she could not place.

She nodded.

"What do you want?" she half whispered.

"I'm here to deliver a message from my boss."

"Who's that?" she asked wide-eyed and feeling dizzy.

He ignored her, and pushed her roughly to the other side of the bed. "Sit down."

She sat, recognizing that she was now within reach of her gun. Her head started to throb and she made to rub it. He grabbed her hand and stood in front of her. He was big, about six feet tall and heavy set. He blocked her view as he filled the space in front of the door. He wore a leather jacket and she noted his pair of sturdy boots.

He leant over her, pushing her flat to the mattress, and with his face inches from hers he said, through clenched teeth. "Don't, I mean, *don't* publish that article. I'm warning you. This is a message from Bruno. If I have to come back, I won't be this nice." He gave her a hard shove and next thing she knew he was flying across the room, hitting the wall next to her dresser, dropping his gun on the bed as he crashed into it causing the mirror on her dresser to shatter. He pushed away from the wall falling towards the bed, reaching for the gun.

Matthew was quicker. He grabbed the gun by the barrel, pushed it aside and struck the intruder on the side of the head. It was not hard enough to put him down for good, but it gave Matthew time to grab him by the coat and lift him upright. He flipped the gun the right way round and aimed it at the intruder's head.

Seething, he said through clenched teeth, "Get out now. Take a message to your boss. If he ever tries anything like this again, he will be hearing from me."

Christina, in the meantime, had recovered and had managed to open the drawer, removing her gun. She was shaking so badly she probably couldn't hit her target. She knew enough not to try.

As Matthew pushed his charge roughly through the door, he looked back at Christina and was astonishment that she had a gun.

Slamming her front door and putting on the deadbolt, he returned to the bedroom. She was still sitting on the bed with the gun in her lap. She was absolutely still. Her face was as pale as the wall behind her.

Moving slowly towards her, softly saying her name as he approached, he gently removed her gun from her grip.

He didn't touch her, he just said her name. His voice registered and she looked at him and as soon as she did she began crying, shaking violently. He wrapped his arms around her and pulled her onto his lap, held her head against his chest and kissed her hair, "Shhush, I'm here now, shush, shussh you're alright, he's gone."

Gradually her crying subsided into sobs. Sniffing loudly, she pushed away from his chest and winced as he looked up into his beautiful but worried green eyes. His shirt was damp. She placed her hand over the damp spot and felt his strong heartbeat. Here he was making her feel safe again, those strong arms surrounding her.

"Are you OK? Did he hurt you? How did he get in here?"

"I don't know, Matthew. Ouch my head hurts!" She touched the back of it gently and winced again. "How does he know what I am writing about? I haven't finished yet. How did *you* know he was here?"

"I didn't. I was lonely. Are you sure you're OK? Let me see." As he examined her head he continued. "I got to your door and it was open. When I got to your bedroom door, seeing that ape standing over you yelling... I didn't see his gun until I pulled him off you. He would have been dead if he fired at you. I would have killed him with my bare hands." He looked into her eyes examining for signs of head injury. "I think you are OK."

She stared at him wondering how she got to be so lucky.

Matthew picked up her gun and unloaded it.

"You never cease to amaze me. Since when have you had a gun? And, I get the impression you know how to use it...

What else haven't you told me?"

Her face reddened under his gaze and she dropped her eyes to her feet. Matthew lifted her chin and she looked into his eyes.

"Christina, tell me what's going on. I need you to fill in the blanks for me. How come I don't know what's going on? We've known each other long enough haven't we?"

She was quiet for a minute rubbing the back of her head. "You haven't exactly been forthcoming about some aspects of your life either, have you?"

"That's not at issue right now, is it? I am not the one in the danger. I know you are very independent and capable, obviously," he said trying not to sound too angry. "When did you acquire a gun and do you really know how to shoot it?"

"Yes. I'm a very good shot, as a matter of fact."

He smiled at her. "You have a habit of omitting certain facts don't you?"

She was relieved, that must mean he wasn't that mad, right?

He pushed her for an answer. "Well, how long?"

"I've had it long before you knew me."

"Why do you have it at all?"

"Well," she said, pausing for a second or two, "I have been alone all my life. I decided that a gun would help make me feel safe, along with my Grav Maga classes. Sometimes assignments are not what they first seem and can be a bit unpredictable, case in point obviously..."

"What else have you omitted? We need to figure out who he works for and how he got in here."

"Not tonight, please, Matthew. I am exhausted and can't think straight. All I need now is you here. Will you stay please, just for tonight? I'd really like that."

"So would I."He helped her stand and led her to the couch, she was still shaking and cold, so he turned on her gas fire. He returned from the kitchen holding a glass of scotch.

"It will help calm you."

She took a mouthful, feeling the hot burst travel down her body.

He took a sip from her glass and handed it back. She declined another sip.

Pulling her onto his lap again, he slowly caressed her back. She began to relax and stopped shivering.

"Matthew..."

"Yes, angel?"

"How do I thank you?"

"You don't have to. I promised I would look after you. I'm just glad I decided to break another promise tonight, though."

"So am I," she said sleepily.

"Come on. Let me put you in bed."

He set her on the bed in the spare room and covered her with the duvet. She pulled his face to hers and kissed him on the mouth and said, "I owe you one."

He returned to the couch, trying to make some sense of the events of the evening as he sipped on the scotch.

As far as he knew there were three people who knew about the article. Where was the missing link?

He found the broom and started cleaning up the mess in her bedroom. Finding her laptop under the bed. It seemed to be in one piece anyway. He made sure he saved her last document and logged off, hoping she had done a backup recently.

Turning to the bedside table, he picked up her gun. Well! And Grav Maga! He knew about that. He reloaded the gun, put on the safety and took it to the living room placing it on the end table next to him. Compared with some of the places he had slept in the past, this couch was quite comfortable. He reached up and snapped off the lamp.

Matthew leapt up, knocking the lamp flying in his haste

to grab the gun on the end table. He stood up and flipped the safety off, aiming at the person who had just touched his leg.

"Matthew, it's me," she yelled, "don't shoot. Ouch that hurt."

"Christ, Christina."

The apartment was bathed in the suffused light of the street lamp filtering through the blinds as he walked toward her. He kissed her forehead.

"How are you? Do you feel better now?"

"No my head hurts but other than that, I'm fine. How about you?" they moved toward the breakfast bar.

"We need to calm down, don't you think. Coffee?"

"Thanks, coffee would be great. I didn't mean to scare you. It's automatic."

He placed the gun on the counter and ran his hand through his hair.

Sitting on the stool he watched her. He could not get over how well she had reacted. Here she was, in her apartment that looked like a tornado had been through it, calmly making coffee.

She sat next to him, placing a steaming cup in front of him and taking a sip from hers. "You, were amazing last night, you know," he said.

"I was terrified. God knows how it would have turned out if..." she kissed his cheek and inhaled. "You saved my life."

"I think you would have found a way to get to your gun and protected yourself. Grav Maga, maybe?"

"Well self-preservation and adrenalin are a potent combination but you know, actually shooting someone! I don't know if I could have done that. It's different when it's just a picture of some evil looking terrorist hanging at the end of a shooting gallery."

"Believe me, angel, I have no doubt that you were capable of that."

"Well let's hope I won't have to find out." Silence ensued.

"Now, Christina, we need to talk, OK?" He looked her in the eye and she flushed, blinking slowly, dropping her eyes to her coffee cup and running her finger slowly round the rim.

Matthew shifted in his seat and turned toward her. He reached out and turned her face toward him, keeping a finger on her jaw.

"What are you not telling me?" he said. "Come on, out with it."

She said nothing.

"I'm waiting, and I'm not going to take silence as an answer."

She removed his hand from her face and held on to it.

"You remember when I first saw you at the bar?" she looked up at him.

"Yes, I remember very well," he said.

"Well, I had stopped there because I was early for a meeting. Well a rendezvous really. I had just begun to research trafficking. First I was distracted by you," she said, kissing the back of his hand. Matthew placed his other hand over them. "And?" he said.

"I received a call, if you remember."

"No I don't actually. I was a little, how shall we say, under the weather that night."

"I know, that's what I kept wondering. What had happened to you that made you so sad? I left for my meeting and you said goodnight and be careful out there, stay safe or something like that. Anyway, my meeting was with an informant. We were to meet under the exit ramp 233!"

Matthew looked at her. "*You* found him?"

"Yes I did."

He glanced at her gun on the counter.

"When I got there, it was spooky. So quiet, all you could hear was the traffic overhead and my footsteps on the gravel and I was scared. I had taken my gun and placed it in the back of my waistband, because things didn't seem quite right.

I moved slowly towards the pillar. I rounded the pillar. He was there. Shot through the head. I pulled out my gun then but to tell you the truth, I probably wouldn't have fired it. How's that for being brave?"

Matthew was silent.

"I had no idea who he was. He had promised it was OK, and he would be safe. He was going to give me names of prominent people..."

"Why didn't you go to the police?"

"I figured if they could kill him, I might be next. I wasn't sure the police could protect me. But I didn't believe they knew who I was, whoever *they* were. There wasn't anyone around, or so I thought." She sighed. "Isn't it funny how things happen. Here we are together. I don't have a clue what to do now but I'm hoping you do."

Matthew put his arm around her shoulder and pulled her to him a slight shiver passed through her.

Eventually she asked, "What do I do now?"

"Well, let's see. You could do what I suggest, stop writing this one." He smiled. "Or we can try to figure out how to keep you safe and get this article published."

Matthew knew which option he preferred, but he knew that wouldn't fly. "First of all, let's get this mess cleaned up."

They spent the next half hour putting everything back in its place in the bedroom, then moved to the living area and began straightening up there. She started with the couch and picked up Matthew's jacket from the floor.

She was folding it and just about to place it on the arm of the chair when she saw something on the carpet next to the upturned lamp. Picking it up she called, "Matthew, come here a minute."

"What's this?" she put out her hand and opened her fist to

reveal a small black object about the size of a penny.

He looked at it and instantly recognized what it was. He took it from her hand, as he pressed his finger to his lips and nodded twice. Reaching for the remote to the sound system he turned on the music, cranking the volume just as he put the object under his foot and stepped hard on it. It broke into several small pieces, then he scooped them up and returned with pen and paper.

DON'T SAY A WORD ABOUT ANY OF THIS JUST CARRY ON AS WE WERE.

She looked wide eyed at him and with a slight tremble in her hand she wrote,

IS IT A BUG?

YES

She spun around raking her hands through her hair as she started pacing and taking deep breaths. Matthew grabbed her by the shoulders. Looking into her eyes he nodded twice, hoping she understood that he wanted them to remain as normal as possible for now. He tightened his grip on her upper arms and gave them a reassuring shake.

She responded with a nod. Moving back towards the kitchen she said, reaching for the coffee pot, "Another cup of coffee?"

"Sure, that would be great," he replied giving her the universal hand signal for OK.

With a shaking hand she poured them a cup. Matthew grabbed her and pulled her to his chest, holding her firmly and kissing her neck he whispered, "It will be alright. I've got you."

After finishing his coffee, he started to look for more listening devices, but not before he wrote, PACK A BAG BRING ENOUGH FOR A FEW DAYS YOU ARE STAYING WITH ME. They left her apartment shortly afterwards.

Scanning the area for anything suspicious, he kept a grip on her arm with one hand and a grip on her gun, inside his jacket, with the other. Removing his gun from the glove compartment he placed it in the console. He gave Christina her gun and told her to keep it in her purse within easy reach, if necessary.

This time there was no black sedan.

He called Dan to set up a meeting at his apartment, saying he would explain then.

Parking in his designated spot, he told her to stay in the car until he reached her door. He stood beside her, effectively blocking access to her from the parking entrance but allowing her free access to the elevator.

Both of them relaxed, somewhat, on the ride to the thirtieth floor. Neither of them said a word. She slid her hand in his, taking comfort in his strong grip.

Passing the security guard at his desk he nodded to him and said, "I will be in touch in a bit, George." He relaxed as he entered his apartment, bolting his door and putting on the alarm system.

Exhaling loudly, he looked at a very pale Christina. "You're safe now, angel, relax. Dan will be here soon and we'll work it out."

Christina finally allowed herself to breath. She felt like she had been holding her breath for hours. All of a sudden she felt exhausted and was in need of a hot bath. She sunk into the couch and just sat there for a few minutes.

Matthew came and kissed her on the forehead and said, "How are you doing now? Alright?"

She put her arms around his neck and slid her fingers into his hair. It was silky and his neck was warm and she just wanted to hold on to him. He crouched down and held her, looking into her eyes. "Would you like a hot shower or a bath?"

"Oh Matthew, how did you know that was exactly what I was thinking?"

He helped her up and they walked to his bedroom where she dropped her bag on the floor. He headed to the bathroom and she heard the water running.

Taking her lounge set out of her bag, she followed him

in. She stopped by the door just to watch him leaning over the tub, testing the water. He had removed his jacket and rolled up his sleeve, his shirt stretched taught over his muscular back. She inhaled, sharply, hoping he didn't hear her.

He turned and said, "Oh, there you are. I'm sorry I don't have any jasmine-scented anything, or even any bubble bath. It's not something I have had occasion to use lately."

She walked over and pulled him to her, brushing his cheek with the back of her hand. "I didn't expect anything like this let alone jasmine-scented anything. You are so kind; I don't even know how to thank you." She kissed him lightly on the mouth.

He returned her kiss. "Anyone would do this for you."

"No one has ever done anything like this for me, ever. How did you know what I needed?"

He shrugged and gave her a peck on the cheek. "Take your time, Dan isn't here yet. The towels are on the heated rack. You know you're safe here, don't you?"

She nodded and he left, closing the door behind him.

Lying in the bath, she finally felt secure. She shut her eyes and all of a sudden she was overwhelmed by the events of the last day and a half. She began to cry. She had held herself together. No way was she going to allow him to see her disintegrate. She had always been strong before he came into her life. Mind you, she hadn't been involved in anything like this. War zones didn't seem as frightening.

Matthew was formulating his approach to Dan when he heard the buzzer to his apartment. Moving quickly to his door he answered the call and buzzed Dan in.

"Matt, what's up? What the hell's going on?"

Matthew, his expression serious, said, "Well, first of all, Christina is here," he pointed to the bedroom.

Dan raised an eyebrow.

"Why?"

"Well, she got in a situation."

"A situation?"

"I suppose I better fill you in. Drink?"

"God no, Matt; it's only the afternoon."

"Oh yes," he said looking at his watch. "Feels like midnight."

He related the events of the night before. Then he filled Dan in on the whole story of Christina's article. When he had finished, Dan looked at him and said, "I didn't realize you two were so involved. I mean after she went to Mexico I thought you had cooled it."

"Sorry, it just sort of happened. Anyway, we have to figure out a way to keep her safe. She will be alright here for the next few days, but I know she won't want to stay for too long, too damned independent, amongst other things!"

The two of them were discussing of the best way to deal with the problem when Christina appeared. She looked better, with more colour in her cheeks, but Matthew noticed her red rimmed eyes. He invited her to sit next to him.

When she was settled with Matthew's arm around her she said, "Nice to see you again, Dan."

"You too, Christina, I hear you're in a bit of trouble."

Rubbing her hand up and down his thigh, she replied, "Yes, Matthew arrived though. Thank God."

Matthew and Dan started to formulate a plan for her safety. They decided to use two of their most trusted and experienced employees.

Their first decision was to send the employees to her apartment, to sweep for more listening devices. Matthew had done a cursory search earlier, and had found one in the phone on her computer desk.

Information would be on a need-to-know basis, as far as the staff went. This would not cause too much speculation, as was often the case with their kind of business.

Christina listened to all of this and interjected occasionally. She gave them some of the information she had gathered but not used in the article. Some was useful but mostly they were working in the dark.

Matthew would contact AJ tomorrow and see what he could glean without getting Christina dragged into his office.

His utmost priority was her.

Chapter 20

For tonight it would be just the two of them. The responsibility weighed heavily on Matthew. He took comfort in the fact that he could pretty much control this environment. He was in a secured building with a guard at the reception in the lobby. He had his own security system. He didn't tell Christina but he had more than one firearm in his apartment. He was on the thirtieth floor, so the only other access would be by, well, he thought for minute, helicopter on the roof, maybe?

He did realize, however, that the person or persons wishing her harm would know by now who he was, if they were worth their salt.

He started to cover all the bases by talking to George at security on the ground floor. Insisting that, should anyone they didn't recognize come in, they were to alert him, even if they did ask for him personally. That was not too difficult, because tenants were required to leave the names of any visitors with security anyway.

Before he had started talking to them, he had asked Christina what she wanted for dinner. She had asked for takeout but he told her no, as that would allow some stranger in to the building. She had not thought of that, so she started looking in his fridge and cupboards.

While she was occupied, he quietly and surreptitiously entered his walk-in closet. Opening a well-hidden door, he removed his gun case and unlocked it. He chose his weapon, loaded it quietly and placed it under his bed. He checked that his sidearm was loaded and the safety was on, then placed it back in the bedside table. He would have put it under the pillow but thinking that Christina will in all likelihood be in his bed tonight, at least if he has anything to do with it, he decided against that location.

He came into the kitchen knowing things were more under control now. He relaxed. Coming up behind her, pulling her to him, he kissed her neck.

Still staring into the fridge she asked, "Do you like risotto?"

"Can you cook risotto?"

"Of course I can," she replied. "I have to eat, you know."

"Yes, I know. I just never thought of you as a cook."

"We have a lot we don't know about each other, haven't we?"

Placing her finds on the counter she started searching for a cutting board and knife. She had found enough ingredients to make a pretty good risotto.

Matthew asked her if she would like a glass of wine and poured her a Merlot. At least he knew what kind of wine she liked.

Leaning back on the counter next to her, sipping his scotch, he watched her moving around his kitchen. It was quite a shock that he actually liked this atmosphere. Even in this stressful situation he felt relaxed, although he was more acutely aware of his surroundings and any strange noises that might emanate from outside. Not much penetrated his penthouse in the way of noise, though.

He noted that she looked a bit better than she had when Dan was here.

He was not going to upset her any more than she already was so he stayed away from their present dilemma. He helped her find the necessary items she wanted for her meal and saw to it that he kept her glass topped up. One scotch was enough for him. Just in case.

After they ate at the breakfast bar, he helped her clear up the dishes, then he took her by the hand and said, "Come on let's sit by the fire." Bringing the wine bottle with him, they settled on the couch.

"This is nice," she said, leaning on his shoulder. "What a day."

He kissed the top of her head and stroked her hair. "How's the head?"

"Fine," she said as she slid her hand inside his shirt.

Matthew was reacting to her touch in other ways, and shifted his position. He didn't want her to think he was insensitive, so he picked up the wine bottle and poured more in her glass. She grabbed him by the shirt front and pulled him. He was taken by surprise and steadied himself before he fell on his knees in front of her, careful to keep a grip on the wine bottle. She planted a hot, long wet kiss on his mouth.

He stayed in that position for several seconds. Having trouble pulling his mouth from hers, he said, "OK, what was that?"

"Oh I don't know," she said, mumbling indistinctly.

He tried to remove her hand from his shirt. He managed, in the end, by kissing her again.

"Come on, I think you have had enough wine for one night."

Her grip loosened.

He placed the bottle back on the ottoman and gently assisted her in getting to her feet. She swayed slightly and he steadied her.

She leaned on him as they walked to his bedroom.

"Can I get your things for you?" he asked, as she sat on the edge of the bed. "Do you mind if I go in your bag?"

"Mmmm... No I don't mind." Her eyes were half closed, and she was thinking she should be getting her own clothes.

Matthew helped her into her nightshirt, and she pulled him to her again and kissed him on the mouth saying, "Don't leave me, please."

Matthew didn't know if she meant don't leave her now, or don't leave ever.

He drew back and looked at her: there were tears in her eyes as he held her to his chest, stroked her hair and whispered, "I'm not going anywhere, angel. Come on, lie down now and sleep, it will be alright."

She lay back on the pillows and he covered her up, kissing her forehead as if she were a child. She smiled and sighed. She was asleep in her next breath.

He stepped back, wondering if she had ever been tucked into bed.

It was still only early evening so he returned to the living room and tried to sort out not only his feelings, but how to keep her safe for the foreseeable future.

He was surprised how outraged he had felt when he found her in the clutches of some ape. He had come across other situations in his career, ones that necessitated swift decisive action, but this one took on a whole different meaning.

He had to admit that he was becoming more and more wrapped up in her. She did things to him that he had not experienced in a long time. His heart melted every time he thought of her dealing with all that life had thrown at her.

On a more practical level, he was sure he could keep her safe. He had the resources to do just that.

Weighing his options, he made some decisions.

It was strange for him to walk into his bedroom and see someone in his bed. Christina was sleeping soundly. She looked angelic, her lips parted slightly, her cheeks flushed in sleep and her hair spread out on the pillow. He wanted to wake her and make love to her. He brushed a kiss over her cheek and gently smoothed her hair on the pillow instead.

He was suddenly wide awake, disturbed by the thrashing beside him. He snapped on the lamp and leaned over to her. She was mumbling and writhing around.

He was not sure if he should touch her. He leaned closer to her, trying to whisper her name in her ear but she kept moving her head away from him, so he spoke more loudly, "Christina, Christina wake up. It's all right I'm here."

He didn't know if she had heard him, so he gently touched her arm. Bad move. She shot up and punched him in the chest and scrambled to the very edge of the bed away from him. Her eyes were wide open and full of fear, but she wasn't seeing him.

Matthew, taken by surprise at the strength of her punch, was taking in a deep breath when she screamed. He scrambled across the width of the bed and, kneeling in front of her, grabbed her in his arms and held on to her tightly. She was no match for his strength even as she began struggling and yelling, "Get away from me, get *away* from me."

He held her head against his chest as tight as he dared.

"It's OK angel, it's OK. I'm here. You're safe, sshh now. Wake up. It's just a bad dream."

Silently, he held her to his chest, kissing the top of her head as her body relaxed and he felt her heart start to return to a more normal rhythm.

He waited another minute before he released her slowly. She took a deep breath. Recognition returned and relief flooded through him. He could still feel the effects of the punch.

"Where am I? What happened? Why are you looking at me like that?" She stared at him, still breathing fast as she wiped the slight sheen of perspiration from her top lip.

"You were having a bad dream. Are you alright now?"

"Yes I think so. Sorry, bad dream about the other night." She looked at him as he rubbed his chest. "What's the matter, are you having a heart attack?" He laughed, "No, darling, you punched me when I was trying to wake you."

Her hand flew to her mouth and she gasped. Her eyes widened as she said, "I did? *Really?*"

"Yes really, you pack quite a punch, you know. Remind me not to get in your way when you feel threatened again."

He leaned towards her, speaking earnestly, "You do know I'll keep you safe?"

"I know, Matthew, but I still find it hard to believe anyone would put their life on the line for me."

"Why not? I do it all the time, and for people I don't even know."

"I am not worth a life," she said, looking at her knees.

"Yes, *you are.*" Then more quietly he repeated his statement.

Christina was near to tears and he moved to her side.

He turned her face to his and looked in her shining almond eyes. "Of course you are. Look what you have tried to do for the exploited of the world."

She put her head on his chest, feeling that wonderful sensation. She kissed the slight reddened area that was the target of her punch. "I'm sorry I hit you, I hope you don't get a bruise there."

"I've had worse than that done to me. Although, I do believe you are the only woman to ever do *that* to me."

She let herself relax into his body. He held on to her and laid her down next to him, pulling her close to his hip. "Let's see if we can get some sleep; we are going to be busy tomorrow."

He shut off the light, and spooned into her feeling very, very comfortable.

The morning was busy, just as Matthew had predicted. He settled Christina in his office with her computer and encouraged her to continue refining her article.

He had a teleconference with Dan and a couple of his staff. He arranged for them to come to his penthouse. He reiterated that they show their ID. He needed them here so that he could go and see AJ. He would drop off a key at Midnight and arrange for one of his specialists to sweep her apartment for more bugs.

When his men arrived, he introduced them to Christina and gave strict instructions to intercept any phone calls.

Christina felt much better. Now, she could concentrate on her article.

She emailed her editor and told him it would be sent by

Friday.

As soon as Matthew reached his office he found it was a hive of activity; on his behalf, as well as Ty's, who, he found out, had run into some more trouble.

As usual everything was being handled. Dan was on the case already. He had made sure that all communication from Ty came to him, leaving Matthew to concentrate on Christina.

He hurried past Anne with hardly a glance in her direction. She knew this behaviour well.

When Matthew had seated himself in his office, he picked up his phone.

"Mum. Hi. How are you?"

There was a long pause on the other end. Then she answered, reticently, "I'm fine… how are *you*? You never returned my call. I was worried." His mother would never stop being his mother.

"I know, Mum, I was having a bit of trouble for a short while there, but it's OK now."

"Well I'm glad that's over. Now, to what do I owe this pleasure?" she said humorously.

Matthew hesitated, then he dove in. "This may come as a shock, but I'm still seeing Christina." He stopped a smile developing as he waited for her response. It took a few seconds before she answered.

"Oh Matthew, that's great, I'm so glad. Is that why you called?" She continued without letting him answer, "When can we meet her? Your father will be so happy for you. We're free this weekend. Bring her to dinner, we would love that. I'll make my famous beef wellington and…"

"Mum, Mum whoa, stop for just a minute. I know you're excited but I have to ask you and Dad something first, alright. Can you get him and put the phone on speaker please?"

She put the phone down and he heard her calling Len.

Soon there was a lot of mumbling going on as they returned to the phone. "Hi son, your mother is gushing about something to do with your girlfriend?"

Matthew smiled to himself. "Yes, Dad, but that's not the sole reason for my call. I need to ask you something very serious. I need a sanctuary for her. I know it sounds strange to ask you that, but it has become necessary for me to protect her. She's not only my girlfriend but she has become one of Midnight's clients. I will explain later. It's too complicated right now but I will say that I will be bringing some of our staff with me. Is the bunkhouse in use at the moment?"

"Well... no... I'm guessing it's quite dangerous for her..."

"Dad, I wouldn't ask you if I didn't think I could keep us all safe. You will like her, I know you will."

"I trust your judgement. Your mother is nodding her approval, so I will say yes but you will have to explain what's going on when you get here. When are you coming?"

"At the moment she is as safe as she can be in my penthouse."

"So when do you think?" his dad asked.

"I have to speak to her then I'll let you know, OK?"

They said goodbye and then he placed a call to AJ. Needless to say he didn't answer, so Matthew left a message asking him to call his cell as soon as he could.

His next plan was a meeting with the security guards he would take with him.

Calling Dan into his office, he told him what his plan might be. Dan thought that it was doable. They set the agenda for his meeting later that day. He was still waiting for AJ to return his call.

Taking a moment to review the agenda, he heard his Blackberry ping. Picking it up, a smile crossed his face. She was complaining already, that the two men at the apartment were a real pain, not letting her out of their sight. Really!! Not answering her own phone? Hell, they only begrudgingly let her send him a text. They followed her to the bathroom for Christ's sake. As he heard her long list of complaints, he knew that taking her to his parents was indeed the right choice.

He texted her back saying that she must behave, and that it would only be for a few more days, he hoped.

After passing the phone begrudgingly to one of the men, she was allowed to open the text. Was there no privacy? She had no idea why it was only going to be a few more days but it placated her bad mood and she resigned herself to waiting for him to return and explain.

Matthew knew he should probably keep her in his penthouse. He was sure he could spirit her away to his homestead. After all he had spirited other people away.

The two men sprang into action at one point, when security called to say that the housekeeper was on her way up. They escorted Christina to the bedroom and one stayed with her while the other let the housekeeper in.

Gracia almost fainted when, after entering, she found herself face to face with the business end of a gun held by a very tall black man in a very nice suit.

She dropped the grocery bag to the floor and stared at the gun with her mouth open.

Hal lowered his gun. "Sorry," he said, "please come in. I didn't mean to frighten you but we have a situation here." He pulled her inside and stopped to pick up the bag, all the while checking the hallway. He closed the door firmly and set the alarm again.

Gracia leaned against the wall and took a deep breath. "Goodness, where is Mr. Bryson?"

She looked to the kitchen and didn't see anyone. Then his bedroom door opened and another imposing figure appeared, also carrying a gun. She started to slide to the floor. Hal grabbed her round her middle and held her up. He carried her to the couch.

When Gracia regained consciousness, Christina was kneeling in front of her. She heard a lovely, kind female voice asking if she was alright. Deciding that she was now dead, she opened her eyes.

A vision, of what she imagined an angel would look like, swam in front of her eyes. When they finally focused, she realized that she was on Matthew's couch and that the voice belonged to a beautiful young woman with long curly hair and almond shaped eyes.

The young woman tried to explain the situation, the two men, the guns, said they were here to protect her, and was about to explain her relationship with Matthew when they heard the lock on the door rattle. Both men reacted fast drawing their guns again, but at the sound of Matthew's voice through the intercom they returned them to their shoulder-holsters. "Relax, fellas. It's me."

He entered, looking as fresh as when he had left earlier on.

His steps faltered as he quickly assessed the scene in front of him. Dropping his keys on the hall table he strode into the living area, going directly to Christina and drawing her to him. "I see it's going well," he said, slightly amused.

Gracia stared at both of them. When had this happened? And how come she didn't know anything about it? She was disappointed.

"Are you alright Gracia, you look a bit pale?"

"I... I'm fine, Mr. Bryson, but I don't understand what's going on."

"It's alright Gracia, these men work for me, and Christina here," he looked at her and squeezed her waist, "needs our help. That's all."

"Well I wish you had warned me, Mr. Bryson."

Matthew took stock of the whole situation and began to manage it. He dismissed Hal and partner, saying he would take over until the morning, then dismissed Gracia, thanking her for the groceries and apologizing for the shock.

As the apartment returned to a state of normalcy, Matthew exhaled loudly.

Christina held him. "Well how was your day?"

"Busy, and productive, except I'm still waiting to hear from AJ. I left him a message this morning."

"Are you sure I won't be arrested for not reporting that murder?"

"I won't let that happen."

"OK, I believe you," she said, kissing his cheek as he took a breath.

"Christina, have you thought this through? What will happen when you send your article to the magazine?"

"I have no idea, Matthew, but I'll tell you one thing, I am not going to back down. After my encounter in Mexico it needs to be published, because it is important. People need to know what goes on."

There was silence as Matthew digested her statement.

"Is it finished yet?"

"Nearly. I would have been further ahead except for the constant interruptions from your, er, men." She sounded irritated.

"Christina, I know this isn't ideal. No privacy and all but you know it's what we have to do. Don't you?"

She sighed. "Yes, I guess so, I just didn't realize how awkward it would be, always having people around. Even if your place is enormous."

"I may have a solution. But we have to wait a few days, until I get things in place. OK. Be patient please."

Wondering what the solution could be, she relaxed.

"The only saving grace about this whole situation is I get to be here with you." She took his hand and kissed the back of it.

Christina went back to his office to do more on her article. Matthew sat in quiet contemplation.

The ringing of his phone returned him to the present. It was

AJ. Matthew would not divulge anything over the phone. AJ was curious to say the least but agreed to a meeting in the morning at his office.

Chapter 21

His meeting with AJ was fractious to say the least. Matthew told him about the home invasion. AJ was furious. He demanded that they at least be allowed to go to her apartment to see if there were any fingerprints. Matthew did not tell him about her rendezvous.

AJ suggested she come to look at some mug shots. Matthew said no. He explained his reasons, that she was safe with him, which surprised AJ as he had no idea they were that close.

Hal and partner were there again, as he had instructed them to be. Perhaps he only needed one of them in his apartment but he could not help being extra cautious.

After his meeting with AJ, he went to his office for another meeting, this time to implement the plan to spirit her away to his parents' house.

Once back in his penthouse, he broached the subject with Christina. "I know this is a bit cloak and dagger, in your estimation, but after speaking to AJ who, by the way, is not happy about any of this but is willing to forgo any action at the moment, I am arranging to take you to my parents."

Christina started to protest but Matthew put his finger on her lips.

"I will be with you and we will have a lot of security there as well. I've spoken to Mum and Dad and they are looking forward to meeting you, even if it is under less than ideal circumstances."

"You always refer to them that way; what are their names?" she said.

"Oh. Leonard and Elizabeth," he said, pointing to a photograph on his mantle.

Christina walked over to it. "I see the resemblance; you are every bit as handsome as him. Except his eyes aren't quite as green as yours, are they? Your mother is beautiful, that's where your chestnut hair came from, I see?" She stared at the photo for a long time, and felt a pang of regret.

Matthew came and stood beside her. Putting his arm round her waist he said, "They are great parents. Even though I am all grown up they still look out for me. Just as they do for my sister. I haven't been myself for a long time but I feel that I am beginning to surface from the darkness that has been my life lately. I have you to thank for that." He turned her head and gently kissed her lips.

There was a sort of wistful longing behind her almond eyes, and all of a sudden he pulled her to his chest and held her there for several minutes.

She slid her hand across his shoulder and down his arm, feeling the hardness of his biceps, and continued on down to his forearm.

She closed her eyes and breathed in – he smelled of body wash and aftershave and, just Matthew. His heart beat a steady rhythm against her chest

"Christina," Matthew said gently, bringing her out of her reverie, "shall we sit or do you want to stay like this for a bit?" He kissed the top of her head and stroked her hair slowly, all the way down to the ends.

She shivered and answered in a whisper, "I could stay like this forever." Matthew gently lifted her up into his arms and carried her to the couch. He set her on his lap and wrapped his arms around her.

She placed her head on his chest once again.

Matthew closed his eyes and inhaled slowly, tightening his embrace. He was concerned about what could happen if he didn't get it right this time. He was checking off his list mentally, making sure he had not missed anything in his preparations for their journey to his sanctuary.

"I've got you. I have your back, angel," he whispered.

She smiled, and sighed contentedly.

The next two days were a whirl of activity, but Christina finished her article. Taking a moment to reflect on all that had happened in the recent past, she steeled herself and, having re-read and re-read it over and over, she pressed send.

Leaning back in Matthew's very comfortable office chair, she stared at the screen for a long time and waited for the sent receipt to pop up in front of her. Once she saw it she felt a bit apprehensive, fearful, one might say, but quickly dismissed that. Matthew came to mind and she smiled to herself. He would keep his promise to her, she was certain. How had she ever lived without him?

Matthew arrived back later than he had expected. Hal and partner were eager to leave once he returned. Matthew was entering and they brushed by him in the doorway. He looked after them, puzzled. "Goodnight Mr. Bryson, see you in the morning."

Turning back to Christina, seated on the couch, he asked, "What's their rush?"

"Oh I don't know, maybe it had to do with me giving them a hard time today."

He spoke on his way past her. "*You,* need to be nice. I have a hard enough time finding good people, I don't need them resigning, now do I?"

He headed for his bedroom to change out of his suit.

He returned, wearing his jeans and a form-fitting t-shirt, no shoes or socks. Christina appreciated every fine curve. The only thing that spoiled it was the gun that he was wearing. She leaned over as he seated himself next to her. She brushed her hand down his arm and touched his shoulder holster.

"Do you have to wear this?" she said kissing him and breathing him in.

"Yes honey, you know I do."

"OK, but... it sort of gets in the way, doesn't it?" she said as she put her arms around him.

"Better to get in the way than not have it when I need it."

She thought about that for a second and hoped he would never need it.

"I promise to not sleep with it on. OK?"

"Scotch?" she asked heading for the bar.

"Just a small one. Thanks."

She sat on the opposite side to his shoulder holster and asked him how the plans were coming.

"We're almost there; another day or two and we will be as ready as we can."

Christina moved closer to him, took his arm and placed it around her shoulder.

"It's going to be OK, you know that, don't you?" Her hand was trembling as she stroked his arm.

Mid stroke his phone rang, making her jump. He leaned forward to retrieved it from the ottoman.

Staring at her reassuringly he answered.

"Hi Sis, I haven't heard from you for a while. No I'm sorry I have been busy this last few weeks... I had a great Christmas..." he winked... "I know, I know I haven't been around for Sara either. I promise I will call her soon. What have you been up to lately? Had any good dates?" He looked directly at Christina and she saw the devilish glint in his eye and heard the teasing in his voice. He became serious again and asked how Sara was, really. He brightened at the reply. "Good, tell her I will be there for her performance. I promise. Bye for now. Give her a big hug from me. Love you both. Speak soon."

He replaced the phone on the ottoman and resumed his position.

"That was Susan, right?"

"Yes, said I would be at Sara's school play. She's an Easter bunny this year."

"You go to all her performances then?"

"Yes I try to."

Chapter 22

Around six o'clock on Saturday morning, two people, a man and a woman, exited the elevator on the parking level of Bentley Towers. They got in a Mercedes SUV with very dark tinted windows and drove out on to the freeway, heading east.

About an hour later two people, a man and a woman, left the same elevator and quickly hurried to a waiting red Lexus. The man was alert and kept his hand close to his gun, which was holstered under his jacket. The woman seemed to be holding her breath, as well as his arm. She adjusted the hat that she was wearing, and pulled the collar of her coat closer to her ears. He leaned over to her and squeezed her hand reassuringly, and said, "I've got your back, angel."

The red Lexus left the parking garage and headed west. The driver was a tall, well-dressed black man. Sitting next to him was his partner. They were alert and settled in for the drive that would normally take an hour but this time would take longer as they were taking the scenic route.

The sun was rising, presenting them with a spectacular, deep red sky.

The quarter horse ranch was a hive of activity, unusual for a Saturday, to say nothing about the owner and his wife. They were up and preparing the guest bedroom for their visitor. She was excited to meet this particular guest, whom she thought may be responsible for the change for the better that she had noticed in her son just recently.

Having prepared the room to their satisfaction, they hurried downstairs and put on the coffee pot. Looking out her kitchen window, she was more than a little perturbed. Men were moving about with military precision. She was curious as to why these precautions had to be taken, but had every confidence that all would be explained when her son arrived with his charge.

Two vehicles appeared in the long sweeping driveway, raising a small cloud of dust as they approached the large, log ranch house. One was a red Lexus. It continued towards the house, while the second vehicle peeled off towards the bunk house, parking in line with all the other vehicles.

Just as the occupants exited the Lexus in front of the ranch house veranda, there was the sound of a faint thrumming in the sky, gradually gaining in strength.

Good. The helicopter passed overhead. Matthew waved at Dan.

His mother was on the veranda waiting expectantly.

His father on the other hand was slightly annoyed at the helicopter, as it was making the horses skittish. He'd have to speak to his son about that.

Matthew rounded the car and opened the door for Christina. She stood with her back to Elizabeth, talking to Matthew.

When Christina finally turned and walked to the veranda, Elizabeth smiled and thought, "Ah yes, Matthew."She then stepped down from the veranda and held her arms to her son, who gave her a hug, kissing her cheek as he whispered, "Thanks Mum."

He turned and, putting his arm around Christina's, drew her forward. "Mum, this is Christina; Christina this is my mother, Elizabeth."

Christina pulled her hat off and shook her dark curls out, her hair falling over her shoulders. At the same time, she smiled and her face lit up.

Elizabeth approached her and instead of taking the hand that Christina was proffering, she hugged her, saying, "Don't be silly – if you are going to be our guest we might as well start off properly. Welcome. I'm glad Matthew got you here safe and sound."

Matthew moved past them, shook his father's hand and

patted him on the shoulder. Leonard grinned, "So, this is her, is it? She's a looker, isn't she?"

Matthew smiled. "Oh yes, Dad, she's that and much more."

The first thing that struck Christina was the size of the beautiful ranch house. It was a log home from top to bottom. Her eyes were drawn to the sweeping wide staircase that led to a balcony overlooking the great room. On most of the walls there were pictures of horses. An enormous fire place was the focal point of the room, with large leather couches set around it. It was sumptuous, yet inviting and comfortable. No wonder Matthew had described his childhood as idyllic. The sun was streaming in, creating a play of light and dark shadows that shimmered on the shiny log walls. Tall windows looked out over an expanse of corrals and white fences, all housing an array of horses.

"Oh, Mrs. Bryson, this is a beautiful house."

Matthew took off his coat, revealing his sidearm and his custom-made grey western shirt and jeans. Completing the outfit were his Justin cowboy boots.

There was a sharp intake of breath from Christina. She had never seen a more handsome cowboy. All he needed now was his cowboy hat.

His mother, on the other hand, was a little disconcerted seeing that he was armed. She refrained from making any comment and started for the kitchen, asking if they would like coffee. Christina followed, replying that she would love one, noting the gleaming granite counters as well as the large island that also served as a breakfast bar set with several high-backed stools.

Matthew took his father aside and explained what was

happening, that he would have to remain armed at all times. His father expressed concern for everyone's safety, mentioned the helicopter and his worries about the horses.

The ranch was buzzing with activity as the security detail set about their tasks.

Matthew felt proud that he had been able, with Dan's help, to put this whole operation into effect. Ever the CEO, he oversaw all aspects and after he had had his coffee, made his way to the center of operations in the bunkhouse across the yard.

Dan and he had developed a plan, one that they were confident would allow his family their freedom to continue their daily lives. Matthew was aware of the danger inherent with this plan, and had sent a decoy car ahead of him, hoping to at least confuse. Christina, not one to enjoy being cooped up, should find this a much more suitable arrangement. Although he wondered how she would adjust to rural life.

Elizabeth took Christina upstairs and showed her the spacious guest room, right next to Matthew's old room. She was somewhat disappointed; after all she had become used to sleeping with Matthew and the thought of being on her own at night made her anxious. She would have to talk to him about that as soon as possible.

She looked around the room. She tested the mattress on the four poster bed, bouncing up and down a few times, pleased with the way it felt, noting with some amusement that there were no squeaking sounds. Spread across the foot of the four poster bed was a handmade quilt in the Lone Star pattern. A comfortable studio couch sat in one corner and in the other a well-appointed bathroom. There was a pine dresser on the other wall, with a large beveled mirror above it. Her window looked out on the back yard, and she could see a couple of barns.

She was still looking out when Matthew appeared. She just stared at him, crossed her arms and hugged herself.

Putting those thoughts aside, she turned to more unpleasant ones. The journey had been quite stressful and of course Matthew had been agitated. Something about that didn't seem quite right.

Christina had no experience of rural life. She found it quite overwhelming. She was used to car horns and diesel fumes and people jostling her on sidewalks. Here, it was peaceful and although not serene, due to the number of activities going on outside, it was relaxing and quiet. She felt her raw nerves begin to calm.

The idea of meeting his parents had unsettled her. She didn't think that she could fulfil their expectations, especially after Vivienne. Here *she* was, with no family. And she was a journalist, for God's sake! She knew nothing of horses. She had only ever seen them in fields or movies. She barely knew one end from another and was intimidated by their sheer size. Secretly, she hoped Matthew would be too busy to introduce her to any of them.

Seeing him returning to the house, she stepped in front of the mirror thinking she looked rather pale compared to all these tanned, healthy people roaming around. So she added a bit more blush to her cheeks and some lip gloss, then finger-brushed her hair. She felt a bit more confident. Halfway down the stairs her eye caught sight of a picture of a horse. She regarded it for a minute; perhaps they were not as scary as she first thought. This one seemed to have a kind expression and lovely eyes. It was being held by a very handsome boy. He wasn't intimidated. In fact, he seemed to be very proud of it. Taking a closer look she suddenly realized she knew that smile. She stroked his picture, and continued on her way. As she reached the landing, jumping down the last step, she landed in the arms of Matthew, who had just entered through the front door. "Whoa there! Where are you going in such a hurry?" He pulled her to him and steadied her till she regained her balance. Her head hit his chest and she looked up at him and smiled: "Sorry, I was on my way to greet you." She stood on her tiptoes and gave him a fleeting kiss on the lips. "Do you know how sexy you look in these clothes and those boots?"

"Well thank you, you look sexy all the time." He brushed a stray curl behind her ear. "Are you settling in? Which room did Mum put you in?"

"The one next to yours..."

"Oh, well. I sort of guessed that might be the case."

"Can you talk to them?" she pouted and in a whisper said, "Please"

"Um... no," he emphasized the no. "Not a good idea. It's bad enough I persuaded them to allow me to bring you here in the first place. Sorry, angel, we will just have to work something out." He turned her around by the shoulders and guided her into the kitchen.

"Smells good, Mum, what's cooking?"

"Homemade turkey soup," his mother answered, stirring the pot. "I hope you like that Christina. By the way, is your room OK?"

"Oh, it's lovely, thank you. Great view over the valley," Christina said.

"How long till lunch, Mum?"

She told him about half an hour, so Matthew said he would go and find Dad and check on Phantom.

"Do you want to come and see him, Christina?" he asked on his way to the back door."Err, no thanks, not right now, I think I will stay here with your mother."

"OK honey, see you in bit," he left, picking up his cowboy hat on the way. He didn't notice her turn pale at the thought.

Christina breathed a silent, "Thank you God."

Left alone, they struck up a conversation about life on the ranch. She learned that Elizabeth had met her husband at university. The were both studying science.

They had been on the ranch ever since they married some forty years ago. Leonard had inherited the farm from his father. It hadn't always been a stud farm, it used to be a cattle ranch but Leonard was more interested in breeding horses.

"Do you like horses?" Elizabeth asked innocently.

"Um, I don't know... I've never really had anything to do with them." Christina hoped that would suffice.

"Oh well, I'm sure Matthew will introduce you to Phantom; he's special in Matthew's eyes." She grinned and continued, "Sometimes I think he loves that horse more than his family."

Christina shifted on the barstool.

"I'm sure he won't mind introducing you two, I'll mention it to him later."

"Oh that's OK. I know he's busy with my situation, so I won't bother him."

She groaned inwardly and wanted to change the subject.

Matthew and his father arrived with Dan in tow. "Hello, Mrs. Bryson, how are you? Sorry I haven't had time to see you before now."

"I hope everything is going OK. Is the bunkhouse all right? Not too crowded."

"No it's fine; we've been in some awful accommodations over the years – this is pure luxury."

"Great, well, anything you need just let Len know, I'm sure we will be able to help." She went back to her soup.

Len and Matthew left Dan and Christina alone.

"How are you holding up?" he asked.

"I'm doing OK, thanks. I hate to be the cause of all this," she said.

"Oh this is what we do. Anyway, Matt insisted and we agreed."

After a short pause Dan continued, "I guess it's sort of in our blood, neither he nor I would be happy paper pushing – we need the adrenalin rush every so often. Besides, Matt and I haven't worked this closely for a long time, brings back some good memories. We really do work well together."

"Some day you will have to tell me your war stories."

They sat in silence. When Matthew and Len entered the kitchen side by side she noticed how they were nearly the same height, with Matthew being slightly taller. Christina watched them, also noting the similarity in their mannerisms and that his father had the same arresting handsomeness, wide forehead and high cheekbones. He was more tanned than Matthew and it highlighted his short silver hair. It was not wavy like Matthew's. His broad shoulders were well developed, and displayed the same strength. She suspected that it had to do with horseback riding. What do they say? If you want to know what someone will look like when they get older, look at their parents. She liked what she saw.

Matthew sat next to Christina at the island, giving her a slight squeeze. She inhaled deeply.

She continued her ruminations on family as she watched his beautiful mother. Christina could tell that she must have been stunning when she was younger. Her chestnut curly hair was shining in the light that streamed into the kitchen. She was a tall woman, about five-eight, slightly taller than Christina. Her body was still shapely, her waist trim, and even though she was the epitome of domesticity, she was fashionably dressed in a pair of well-fitting jeans and a black cashmere sweater. Her makeup was not overstated and her lip gloss gave just a hint of colour to her lips. She wore a pair of small emerald studs in her ears. Christina wondered if that was why Matthew had given her emeralds.

So here she was surrounded by the obvious love of a close family, who all seemed so happy to be together and who had welcomed her without reservation. She felt as comfortable as if she had known them forever and it had only been a matter of hours. What would it be like to actually belong to this family?

The turkey soup was delicious. Matthew and Dan left to go and brief some more men.

Christina helped Liz with dishes – "Anything else you need help with?" – and was told everything was under control for supper.

She went out to sit on the veranda.

It was warm enough, no need for a coat, if you sat in the sun.

She watched Len as he left to check one of his brood mares who was due to drop a foal any day.

Christina sat in the Adirondack chair. She closed her eyes and concentrated on the new sounds and smells surrounding her. The sun was warm on her face and seemed to penetrate to her very soul, just like the atmosphere that prevailed within this ranch. She absorbed it.

She was brought back by the sound of footsteps on the veranda and someone blocking the sun.

Matthew stroked her face and leaned in to kiss her. She squinted up and smiled, kissing him back."Everything alright?"

"Oh yes, Dan does a good job. We are ready for all eventualities." He eased into the chair next to her.

"No wonder you have such nice memories of this place, it is idyllic. I love it. I'm more relaxed every hour. I feel safe here."

"Good. That was the whole idea. Now, when is that article out? Once it is, I think you should be out of harm's way. The damage will be done. There's little point exposing themselves to the police and an investigation."

"It's due on the shelves in two weeks," Christina said. "Can we stay here that long? Your Mum and Dad won't be too upset will they?"

"They both love you already. Imagine how much more they'll like you after two weeks of getting to know you."

"I don't think I can stand two weeks sleeping alone."

"We'll just have to grin and bear it, OK? We can manage two weeks, right?" She thought she heard him groan a little.

"Come for a walk with me, please Matthew; I want to go running some time, so maybe you can show me around. Can I do that here?" she said.

"I'll have to let Dan know. Not alone, mind you, but I think it will be alright. We'll see tomorrow."

He uncurled himself with ease and rose, pulling her out of the chair, pulling until she was pressed against him. He kissed the top of her head and she kissed his chest, leaving a smudge of lipstick on his shirt. "Damn, I've left a mark," she said, looking apologetically at him.

"I'm marked now, so that means I'm yours, right?"

"Oh yes, I hope so!"

He directed her towards the barn. "Do you want to go a different way?" he said, holding his hand out to her.

"Um, no it's alright, but we're not going inside are we? After all I can't run in there... can I?"

"No, but you could see Phantom."

"Oh, it's such a nice day... perhaps I'll see him another time. Let's walk." She pulled him away from the barn all the time kissing him on the mouth, which was difficult as he was so much taller than her, even more so in his boots. He almost had to lift her off the ground.

Matthew led her down the trail he sometimes used with Phantom, telling her that this was the only acceptable route, as it was in view of all the security posts. It was also quite smooth. They walked the length of the trail until it petered out just before the trees on the perimeter of the pasture. They were unhurried and stopped to kiss frequently.

Christina was delighting in the leisurely stroll but every time she came in contact with the cold steel of his gun she was reminded of the reality of their situation. She could not believe that she was involved with this cowboy, CEO, hero! Surrounded by the gun-toting testosterone-fuelled men hanging around every corner. The mind-blowing thing to her was that they would be willing to fight or even die for her and she didn't even know them.

After a fantastic beef wellington, Dan and Matthew excused themselves and made their way to the bunkhouse for an update.

As night began to fall, there was an increase in the activities outside the ranch house.

Christina helped Elizabeth with the dishes and soon they were seated in the great room, in front of the fireplace. Christina was feeling very comfortable. Matthew's parents were easy to talk to and didn't push her for any details on her relationship with their son. She was thankful for that.

She began to fully realize that she had never experienced anything like the love that was so evident in this home. She knew Matthew was different from anyone she had ever met before. Now she understood part of the reason why.

When he returned he joined her on the couch. He leaned back put his hand on the back of the couch, stroking her hair casually as he crossed his ankle over his knee.

His parents exchanged a knowing glance and Leonard stood and asked if anyone wanted a drink. Matthew declined. Christina and Elizabeth asked for a Merlot and Leonard had a bourbon and branch.

"How are things out there?" his father asked.

"Everything is under control."

"Great. No need for me to worry then, right? I did get the hands to stable the horses tonight though. I thought it best." He sipped on his drink.

"No worries, Dad, I have a guard outside the large barn."

Looking at Christina, he asked, "How are you doing honey?"

She wanted to touch him and kiss him but thought better of it, so she looked at him and smiled instead. "I'm fine. So everything is going well, is it?"

"Yes. I've got your back." He kissed her lightly on her blushing cheek.

His father rose, "Well, I think I'm going to do a check on that brood mare before I head to bed." And pretty soon his mother left.

Matthew smiled at them knowingly. He kissed his mother on the cheek, whispering, "She's great, isn't she?" Squeezing his arm, she left the room.

Matthew moved to the fireplace, looked at Christina. "Well, what do you think?"

He sounded proud and Christina looked at him and just let herself admire his silhouette as he stood there; his emerald eyes were even more intense than before, his chestnut hair only served to enhance them. She couldn't decide if she liked him better in his beautiful suits and ties or like this, all casual.

The electricity crackled as desire washed across Matthew's eyes. He shifted his stance as she moved towards him.

"Stop. I'm standing here for a reason, Christina." She slowed her advance. He said, in an almost inaudible, husky voice, "I will not break another promise, especially here. I told you, we had to behave. OK?"

She stopped and drew in a deep breath, "I'm sorry. I guess I forgot."

He stayed motionless and replied, "I know. I feel the same, believe me."

With a herculean effort, she managed to turn away from him. Reaching the stairs, she stopped and turned back. "Not even a good night kiss?" she said provocatively.

With his hands still in his pockets and a look so hot she almost fainted, he said, breaking into a grin, "Come here." He held out his arms, inviting her in. She rushed across the room. Reaching up, grabbing his shirt front and pulling him to her, she kissed him fast and hard on the mouth. "Good night, Matthew. I love you." Then she was gone.

Christina made it to her bedroom. She sat on the bed and tried to calm herself. Once she had achieved that, she donned her night attire, and reached for her Blackberry. She hadn't had much need for it today but if he was not going to be with her tonight, she figured a poor substitute is better than no substitute.

Lying propped up against her headboard, she was fully aware that just on the other side of the wall was Matthew's head board, only literally inches apart but, in reality, unreachable.

Matthew was heading to his room when he felt the vibration in the breast pocket of his shirt. He read her text.

You looked so hot, you can't imagine how hot I feel right now.

Don't tempt me please.

Are you sure that you don't want to replace B.O.B.?

Who?

My battery operated boyfriend.

He had no idea how to answer that, so he waited a moment.

I am carrying a gun remember!! Be good and go to sleep, please.

So he was not playing tonight. Disappointed, Christina placed her phone on the bedside table.

She heard his footsteps hesitate as he passed her door. She looked expectantly towards it. Lying in the dark, she heard his shower start. It ran for a very long time.

Matthew felt somewhat better after his prolonged shower. He knew it was going to be a long night.

He slept fitfully. Fleeting dreams, small snippets of what he wanted to do with her, invaded his dreams, causing him to become restless, hot and sweaty. He spent most of the night wrestling with his bedding, occasionally moaning softly.

Sometime during the small hours of the morning, the headlights of a vehicle played on the ceiling of both their rooms.

Matthew heard it. He wasn't alarmed.

Christina heard it and was alarmed. She wondered if she was safe. She lay quite still, her heart pounding. She heard the faint thud of the car door and the mumbling of conversation and waited for something to happen. It didn't.

Eventually she concluded this was no threat, just part of the security detail outside, of course. She grabbed one of her pillows and held it to her chest. Her thundering heart slowed as she drifted off to sleep.

Matthew stayed awake. He had complete confidence in his organization's capabilities and the plan that they had in place.

Eventually he slept.

At least, he thought he did. A vision appeared beside him. He heard her beautiful soothing voice say, "*It's alright Matthew, I understand*" and she stroked his cheek then her image faded slowly as it drifted towards the window.

All of a sudden he was aware that he was standing in front of his window. He was awake but he was not sure how he got there. Looking out at the stars, he felt a familiar sensation, one that made his eyes blur. His hand went softly to his cheek and he stood there for a long time.

Chapter 23

The morning dawned bright and warm. Christina was awake early. Well, in fact she had not slept much. She put on her running shoes and her jacket and made her way downstairs. She was surprised to see everyone in the kitchen already.

Matthew had his back to her when she entered; her eyes went to the gun on his hip.

"Good morning. Isn't it lovely out today?"

He turned and his face brightened briefly before he registered her attire. "Yes it is, are you planning on going for a run?"

"Yes, is that alright?"

"Christina, honey, you must tell me or Dan when you decide to do these things. We can't protect you if we don't know where you are." He held her gaze and gently gripped her by her arms. "Please let us know. Now if you could just wait a minute I will come with you." He left, talking to someone on his phone. She didn't know who.

He returned dressed for running" OK. It's all set. We can go now, if you're ready."

They promised not to be that long, breakfast would be about an hour. She noted he looked tired and a feeling of guilt stabbed her conscience but she was so happy to be close to him again. They stretched out a bit in the back of the house, before setting out across the yard on their way to the trail they had walked yesterday. Falling into an easy rhythm beside each other she asked him if he was alright.

"I didn't sleep that well, how about you?" he said, concentrating on the path ahead.

"Me neither," she said. "This sleeping apart thing is harder than I thought."

"I know but it's even harder if you keep tempting me." He smiled his disarming smile.

"I will have to confiscate your phone if you don't stop."

"You would do that! Seriously."

"I most certainly would."

"Oh," was all she could manage in reply.

They ran to the end of the trail and stopped for a breath. She pulled him to her, kissing him slowly. He didn't return her kiss.

She broke away and looked at him curiously, "Matthew, what's wrong?"

"Nothing but, you do know that we are being watched." He swept his gaze around the pasture.

"What!" she said alarmed. "Are we OK? Where are they?"

"It's OK, it's OK. They are from Midnight. Remember, I told you yesterday." He laid his hand on her and felt the slight tremor in her arm. He rubbed his hand down her forearm, leaving a trail of heated skin in its wake.

"Christina, don't be so nervous, it's OK, I am here and, so are they. I've got your back, remember."

He pulled her to him and held her tightly.

The trembling ceased almost immediately. They stayed like that for a minute or two, in silence. When he was sure she was alright he released her and stepped back. "Are you alright now?"

"Yes I'm fine now. Let's go back, we don't want to be late."

As they were returning, the sound of helicopter rotors reached them. Matthew looked up and said, "Good morning Dan."

The helicopter swept low and they were caught by the wash. Dan waved from the cockpit and Christina looked up and took a certain amount of comfort as it headed out towards the woods.

They returned just as Elizabeth was stacking the pancakes on a large platter.

"Don't be too long," she said as they went upstairs to shower, separately.

Wearing another beautiful western shirt, this time in brown, and smelling as delicious as ever, he returned to the kitchen before Christina did.

His mother kissed his cheek. She noted the unusual dark circles under his eyes and asked if he slept well.

"Not really, Mum, but that's OK. Where's Dad?"

"He's in the barn with Jake; they went to check on the mare, she dropped the foal last night."

"Oh I'll have to take Christina to see it. I don't think she has much experience with this sort of thing."

Just then she arrived in the kitchen. "I don't have any experience with what?" she asked, looking between them.

"Horses and foals, honey," he said.

"No, I'm afraid I'm a city kid," she said.

"Well, you should be able to see the new foal soon. Would you like that?"

"I'm not sure. I think I am a little intimidated by horses..." She looked at Matthew.

He looked at her for a second and then said, "We'll see what we can do about that."

She smiled at him and turned her attention to the pancakes.

Leonard arrived in time for breakfast, saying that Morning Star's foal was perfect.

Addressing Christina, he told her that Morning Star was very experienced, as this was her fourth foal and she was an excellent mother. They decided to wait a couple of days before he took Christina to see them.

The next two days she and Matthew were still behaving themselves, but just barely. Desperate kisses and heated caresses were all that happened between them. On the third day his

Mercedes arrived, out of the blue. One day it wasn't there and then the next it was. Christina only noticed it when she crossed the yard on her way to the running trail. When had that appeared?

After he had spent most of the day in his father's office, attending to business with his own office Matthew came to find her.

She was on the veranda reading her book.

"Hey! How are you? I haven't seen enough of you today."

She looked up at him, squinting against the sun. "I was on the verge of coming to find you."

"Well, here I am; let's go for a ride."

"What, on a horse?" she said, fearfully.

"Oh no," he laughed, "I wouldn't do that to you yet. We haven't even showed you a horse close up, have we? I meant a drive."

"Well sure I would love that, but where are we going?"

"I'm going to show you this property, and we are going to have some alone time."

At last, she thought.

He drove down the road for a short while and then made a turn onto a dirt road. He slowed down and pointed ahead. "This," he swept his hand across the horizon, "as far as the eye can see, is it."

Christina couldn't believe that all she saw ahead of her was his father's property. No wonder he maintained a helicopter.

They drove along the dirt road, kicking up dust. Fields stretched out either side of them, some had cows in and some had horses and some had nothing at all. He kept going for quite some time, and as he began to climb a small hill a magnificent view was revealed before their eyes. Rolling hills swept into a valley and on the horizon were mountains bathed in a blue haze against the backdrop of an almost clear blue sky.

"OK Dan, I've got it from here." He pulled his ear piece out and dropped it on the dash.

She looked at him incredulously. "Where is Dan?"

He leant forward, looking through the windshield and pointed up into the sky.

"Up there," he said, amusement reflected in his voice.

"I didn't know we were being followed." Then she heard the familiar sound of the helicopter.

"That's the whole idea of surveillance, honey."

Coasting slowly down the hill into the valley below, he pulled to a stop next to the river bank, close to a cottonwood tree, and turned off the engine.

"This is my favorite place. It's great for just sitting and enjoying."

He got out and beckoned her to follow. Jumping out, she caught up to him and grabbed his hand eagerly. He lifted her down the last few feet of the bank, clutching her close to him and kissing her before he set her on her feet. She followed him to a grassy spot and he sat down, leaning back on the trunk of a tree, patting a spot beside him.

He crossed his impossibly long and sexy legs at the ankle, displaying his even more sexy cowboy boots again. She leaned on his shoulder and breathed in, revelling in his scent.

Neither of them said a word. They drank in the sounds and the smells.

Matthew's pulse was quickening. He felt her heat next to him and heard her short breaths. He leaned over and placed a deep passionate kiss on her hot quivering lips.

She sighed and explored his lips with her tongue. He let her in and then their tongues were sliding over each other and sucking and they were gasping in air. If they hadn't pulled away the bark on the tree would probably have ignited.

"That's better," he sighed, "but I have to stop now."

He relaxed against the tree, pulling her to him, keeping his arm around her shoulder. She leaned into him silently just gently stroked his chest, feeling his fluttering heartbeat. He adjusted the holster on his hip and eventually said, "Let's go back to the car, I have a surprise waiting there."

He rose with ease, pulling her up by her hand, helping her climb the bank.

Her curiosity was getting the better of her as she waited to see what he had thought of now. He passed his foot under the rear bumper and the back of the SUV opened slowly.

"Close your eyes," he said.

Once it was fully open, he said, "OK, you can open them now."

He put his hand around her shoulder, extending his free hand with a sweeping gesture.

She was surprised. There was a cooler plugged into his car and it was humming gently and a basket holding all the necessary things needed for a picnic, as well as a large blanket that was folded neatly to one side.

"Oh! I had no idea. This is great. You think of everything. Thank you." She stood on her tip toes and kissed his cheek.

They spread the food on the back of the Mercedes and spread the blanket on the ground. He allowed himself one glass of wine as they enjoyed the impromptu smorgasbord. Matthew seemingly had thought of everything, even choosing a satellite music station. He turned up the volume, and they settled on the blanket, stretched out next to each other with a plate of food between them, feeding each other cheese and grapes. This was the most relaxed he had been since arriving. They laughed and told each other silly jokes. Matthew related some of his more memorable horseback riding incidents.

When they had eaten their fill, he said, "I suppose I have

to come clean; I didn't do all this myself. I was in the kitchen putting it together, Mum asked me what I was doing, she took pity on me and prepared this. She said she hoped that you would like it."

Christina smiled, looking into his eyes, saying, "But the idea was yours and that is all that counts. Thank you and I will thank your mother. You are just what a girl needs." She pulled him to her feeling the soft warmth of his neck and ran her fingers into his hair as she brushed her lips over his.

He adjusted his gun on his hip in order that he might lean closer

"Matthew, can you take it off, please?" she said, touching the holster.

"Why?" he asked mischievously.

He unclipped it from his belt and laid it on the blanket.

He pulled her over on top of him and kissed her. "You are my undoing, you know. What shall I do with you?"

"I am in need of some real loving."

She kissed him hard and placed her arms on either side of his head, stroking her tongue down over his pulse, feeling it quicken and then whispered in his ear, "Please", in her most alluring voice.

He groaned a desperate groan.

He lifted her slightly, placing her more comfortably on top of him.

"God, please forgive me." He rolled her to his side and slid his hand under her shirt, caressing her spine.

He pressed her to him, warmth melding his body to hers, and it was his undoing.

They entered the driveway just as his Blackberry buzzed.

Parking by the veranda, he pulled his Blackberry from his

pocket. He listened intently then headed towards the bunkhouse, leaving Christina to wonder what was going on.

Just as she was beginning to feel secure, she was feeling on edge again.

Matthew arrived back in the house and sought out his father, who was in the kitchen helping his mother. "Dad, can I see you for a minute?"

"Sure, let's go to my office."

Christina looked anxiously after them and made her way to the kitchen.

Matthew gave Len the unsettling news.

"May I help you? I see you have lost your helper," Christina said as she picked up the dirty dishes from the counter.

"That would be nice," Liz said with a smile.

"I'm sorry I'm causing so much trouble, Liz. I told Matthew not to do this but he insisted that it would be alright with you both."

"Oh Christina, don't give it another thought. It's fine. I see how Matthew looks at you. I only ever remember one person who got the benefit of that look before."

"He doesn't talk about her very much," Christina said a little wistfully. "I wish he would. I feel like I'm living with a ghost sometimes"

Elizabeth stopped what she was doing and looked at Christina, "Oh honey, he has to be the one to tell you about Vivienne but I will say that he was nearly destroyed after she died. I didn't know if he would ever recover. I look at him today and all I can say is thank you for bringing the sun back into his life. You are the best thing for him. He is more like the Matthew we all know and love."

"He is the best thing that has happened to me. I don't know who has saved who, but I will do my best to keep him happy. By the way, thank you for the picnic. It was lovely"

Len and Matthew returned, looking concerned. Matthew went to Christina and kissed her cheek.

She kissed him back, noting the tension in his face. She touched his arm and his biceps were knotted and as tense as she had ever felt them.

She looked into his eyes, "Is everything alright?"

He answered, rather too quickly, she thought, "Yes, Yes everything's fine."

He pulled her to him and held her tightly to his chest. She could hardly breathe. Once again she felt the butt of his gun against her hip. She trembled, slightly. He felt her tremble and squeezed her momentarily.

He released her and said cheerfully, "You know Morning Star and the foal? It's a filly and she is beautiful just like you. Same colour as your hair. I'll take you to see her in a day or two. I think we need a distraction, right Dad?" He looked at his father who smiled a reply. "We certainly do. We, certainly do."

He addressed Christina "Well, we're going to have to come up with a name soon. I'll have to register her," he said.

"Perhaps you have some ideas."

"Oh, I don't know about that. Hell, I don't even have a cat," she said laughing.

Suddenly the tension in the room had disappeared and they all took a deep breath. Matthew's heart swelled and warmth spread through his entire body.

They rose as one and said they had things to attend to, Leonard heading to the barn and Matthew to the bunkhouse.

Dan had eaten his supper in the house with them and had left shortly after, not taking the usual time relaxing and shooting the breeze with Matthew's Dad.

Christina was left on her own in front of the fireplace.

The logs shifted sending sparks upwards. She followed them as they escaped up the chimney, her thoughts fleeing as she was interrupted by the front door opening as a cold blast of air reached her. She turned and saw Matthew adjusting his holster as he said, "It's cold out there tonight." He looked around. "You're all alone here?"

"Have you been outside all this time?" She rubbed his arm.

"I was just doing a check on the security detail."

She snuggled up to him and felt him warming up against her arms. He kissed her again. "That's better," he said as she snuggled closer.

"Thank you for the picnic and the loving. A delightful new experience, I must say." She kissed the back of his hand, clasped it between both her hands, kissing each one of his fingers.

They both heard the helicopter fly overhead and she held him a little tighter.

"Is something going on that I should know about?"

"No, Christina, everything is going to be fine."

She didn't believe him.

Staring into the fireplace together they sat in each other's silence.

Christina heard his heartbeat, steady and strong, as she rested her head on his chest. Apprehension melted away as she absorbed his scent and his strength. He exuded confidence. She placed her arms around his waist and held him tightly.

Matthew spoke first. "You seem very nervous again tonight. Don't be. I will keep you out of harm's way." He stroked her hair and kissed the top of her head.

"I know you will, but I'm scared something might happen to you," she said quietly, her lips touching his shirt.

"Nothing's going to happen to me. Come on it's late."

He stood up, pulling her with him. He stopped outside her

room, pulling her into a kiss, sighing, "Goodnight."

Outside, some distance from the house, a vehicle was making its way down a dirt road guided only by the light of the almost full moon. The occupants wished the clouds would clear, as they were intermittently plunged into total darkness, leaving them to guess the direction the road took. They were looking for a specific building on the edge of a pasture, hidden from view by a few trees, and some thick brush.

CHAPTER 24

Both Christina and Matthew were woken from their fitful sleep by the sound of the heavy rain slashing against their windows and a strong wind. It was strong enough to cause Christina to switch on her bedside lamp and get out of bed. Pulling on her robe, she went to the window and pulled the shade up, watching the rain bounce off the barn roof and form large puddles in the back yard. She saw the lights of a jeep that approached and parked in front of the bunkhouse and saw two men who hurry inside. She felt sorry for them, out there in that weather, all because of her.

Closing the blind, Christina decided to make her way quietly down to the kitchen.

After pouring the boiling water she moved to the fridge for the milk, and was turning to sit down when she almost jumped out of her skin, coming face to face with her handsome lover seated on the other side of the counter.

"Oh god, you gave me a fright. I didn't hear you coming."

"Sorry, I wasn't supposed to be heard. I didn't know who it was down here, I came to investigate," he said, placing his ever present gun on the counter next to him.

"Come here," he said. She took his hand and rounded the counter. He pulled her in between his legs and wrapped his arms around her. "Is that better? I could almost hear your heart beating from over there."

"Yes, it's always better here." Her hands were on his bare chest.

"The storm woke me, how long were you there?"

"Long enough to admire your sweet derrière." He squeezed her behind.

"Well, I would have liked a heads up. I nearly had a heart attack."

He sipped her tea, "Mmm... good; can I have one?"

She made him a tea then she seated herself next to him

and started drinking. Her gaze was distracted by the gun.

"I feel sorry for your men, out there tonight. It's awful."

"Don't be. They're fine. Just take comfort in the fact they are there and you are safe in here. Although I'm glad it's them and not me out in that rain. The perks of ownership," he said impishly.

The next morning dawned bright and clear. The air was clean and refreshing as Christina and Matthew went running along the trail. They ran in unison and the slap of their feet on the wet trail echoed around them.

They returned famished, but showered quickly. After breakfast, Matthew said, "I think Morning Star is ready to show off her baby. Put on your boots, we'll go and see her."

Hesitantly she obliged; she would not let Matthew know how she felt. She had come to the conclusion that she was becoming too dependent on him and it was time for her to take back her independence, so she feigned excitement.

Matthew led her out through the back door and across the yard to the big barn. She held his hand firmly, but not too firmly. He slid the big door open with one practiced hand and Christina was taken by surprise – she thought it would smell awful. It didn't.

He walked her down the center of the barn, passing large pens, or as Matthew would call them, loose boxes, each holding a horse.

The horses were curious, some of them snuffled and some of them shuffled their hooves on the floor, creating a sharp clang that made Christina gasp. And some of them came over their doors in order to get a better look. Christina was unprepared for their size and her heart began to beat a little faster and her grip become a little tighter.

He removed his hand from hers and put it protectively around her waist. "It's alright, they won't hurt you. They are used to people, in fact they love attention." He raised his hand to one of them as he was passing by and rubbed the end of its nose with the back of his hand. "See, he likes that."

The further down the barn they progressed the more she relaxed. By the time she reached the box with Morning Star, she didn't notice the barn smell at all.

"Wait here," he said. She stood back.

"Now I'm going to open this door. It's OK, she won't come out so just stand still."Christina did just that. In fact, she was holding her breath as well.

He entered the stall quietly, closing the door behind him. It was quite high and all she could see was Morning Star's head and neck and Matthew's head and shoulders. He was speaking quietly to Morning Star. Christina couldn't really hear what he was saying but she guessed it was working, as Morning Star moved to him and nudged his chest.

"Whoa, old girl, I'm here to show off your baby." Bending forward, he disappeared from Christina's view.

He straightened up and that's when Christina could see he was holding the foal in his arms. The foal's head was level with his shoulder and her eyes were big and dark brown, her ears pricked forward. Christina had never seen anything quite so beautiful.

Matthew walked to the door with the foal. Morning Star watched warily.

"Do you want to stroke her? She won't hurt you."

"Can I? Are you sure her mother won't mind?"

"Nah, Star's used to me, and besides we aren't taking her anywhere. Come here."

Christina stepped forward and Matthew raised the foal higher. Tentatively she put her hand over the door, touching the foal's ear, then she stroked between the eyes with the flat of her hand. She was surprised at how soft the hide was. She had expected it to be coarse. When she got to the foal's nose, there was no-one more surprised than she to discover that it was like velvet.

Matthew watched Christina intently. Knowing that she was apprehensive, he had stayed inside the stall, not wanting to frighten her any more than she already was. He wanted her to grow to love horses the way he did. Matthew set the foal down and came out.

"Not bad for a city kid. How did that feel?"

"I didn't know what to expect. Not nearly as intimidating as I thought it would be."

"Well that's enough for today. Perhaps tomorrow we will introduce you to Phantom."

"I think I might like that."

She put her hand behind his back and slid it in his back pocket, and they walked out of the barn together.

"Where is Phantom kept?"

"Over there." He indicated to a much smaller barn to the right side of the house.

"Oh. How many horses are in that one?"

"Mine, Mum, Dad's and a pony that we keep for Sara, who's only five."

Christina pulled him to her side and said, "I think you are probably her favorite uncle."

Matthew smiled and said, "I'm her only uncle."

On the way by the smaller barn, Christina wondered how tomorrow would go. She was less apprehensive now that she had plucked up the courage to go to the barn, and she knew Matthew would not force her into something she did not want do, so she was excited to test herself.

Matthew headed to the bunkhouse. She went to her room, texted her editor and asked how everything was going with the article.

He replied "Fine," said there seemed to be a lot of interest in it, so he was happy. It would be on store shelves next week. She hoped Matthew wouldn't be too long.

The next day was a revelation.

Matthew took her to the small barn. She knew immediately which horse was Phantom. He commanded attention the minute they entered the barn, being the biggest horse there. He held his head high as he came over the stall door. When Matthew came in, Phantom greeted him with a snort.

Christina stood with her back against the wall as Matthew opened the stall door and stepped in. She had never been so captivated by the beauty revealed before her. Phantom's coat gleamed, like it had been waxed, and his mane was glinting in the sun that streamed in the window of his box. His tail was long and straight and he had one white ankle. He was brown, bordering on chestnut, the colour of Matthew's hair.

She thought Matthew was tall and imposing but he looked small in comparison. Phantom's back was nearly as tall as Matthew. Matthew pushed Phantom, causing him to take a few steps back and tied him by his halter. He obeyed the command to stand still. Matthew beckoned Christina. When she stepped toward him he walked behind her placing both hands on her waist. His body touching her back he said, "He won't hurt you."

There was nothing between her and Phantom now and she was a little scared, but took comfort in the feeling of Matthew pressed against her back. Matthew walked her forward and said, "Steady Phantom," then put his hand over Christina's shoulder and held Phantom's head by the halter. "Here, touch him," he said gently in her ear. He took her hand and proffered it towards Phantom's nose. Phantom, all the while, was looking down his nose at her, seemingly assessing her. Taking a deep breath, she allowed Matthew to place her hand on Phantom's nose. She felt the velvet of it and the soft warm breath waft over her hand as his nostrils flared, but Phantom just stayed still, allowing her to touch him.

Once she had done that, she relaxed and became more daring, moved her hand to his cheek and slowly stroked downwards. Then she touched his neck and followed its curve towards his shoulder. Her hand was flat against him, feeling his powerful muscles. His skin was warm and soft. Something seemed to flow from him to her and all of a sudden there was no apprehension. It melted away as if Phantom had invited her into his world.

Matthew had stepped back. He held on to the halter and let her continue her discovery,s delighted at her reaction. Christina ran her hand slowly along the length of Phantom's back towards his tail and over his rump, then ran it down his hindquarter to his leg. She straightened up and turned towards Matthew, her face glowing and her eyes bright and wide. Placing her hand on Matthew's chest, she said, "Now I understand; I have never experienced anything like this before. Thank you." She stood on tiptoe and kissed him as he embraced her. "I knew you would be alright," he said.

Phantom would not be denied his affection either; he nuzzled Matthew's shoulder and Matthew and Christina laughed. "OK, Phantom, don't be jealous; you'll have to share now," Christian said, placing her hand on Phantom's neck.

They left the barn with their arms around each other, Phantom whinnying after them.

"Later, Phantom," Matthew said. "I promise I will ride you today, but right now I have some work to do."

Walking into the tack room she was astonished to see all the saddles and bridles each in its assigned spot with a name plate for each horse above the tack. It smelled of saddle soap and leather. The saddles all had various patterns stamped into them. Christina thought they were beautiful.

Matthew walked into his father's office just as Leonard was concluding a phone call. He sat in the easy chair next to his father's desk.

Leaning back, looking every bit as handsome as his son, wearing a western cut denim shirt and jeans, Leonard said that he had just received a call from a potential client looking to use his stud services. Arrangements had been made for a meeting.

"It's a new client," Leonard said, quite pleased. "A Mr. Calderone."

"Well, I'm glad they thought of you. That ad in the Quarter Horse has paid off. You've had a couple of new clients from that haven't you?"

"I guess I have."

Changing the subject, he appraised Matthew.

"You look very pleased with yourself. How are things? That girl of yours, is she coming around about horses? She seems so tough but I was surprised she wasn't eager about going to the barn yesterday. She didn't cry off, did she?"

"No, Dad. She just needed a bit of encouragement. Once she was there, I showed her the foal and she fell in love with it. You can always count on baby animals. We saw Phantom this morning."

"Oh, how did that go? Did Phantom behave?" His father was smiling.

"Dad, the most extraordinary thing happened. Phantom

was on his best behaviour. I have never seen him so obliging. I can't tell you how happy I am. I thanked Phantom and promised him I'd take him for a ride today."

"Great, Matthew. Just great. Next step?"

"I hope I can get her on one soon."

Matthew's Blackberry buzzed and he checked the caller ID. "I have to take this, Dad." He moved to the window, answering as he went. "Yes, I can come into town. How about tomorrow?" He paused. "Yes that's fine. See you then. Oh, by the way, thanks for this."

"Oh, going into town tomorrow?" his father said. "Can you pick me up a few things? I can't go, as that client is coming."

She spent part of the morning reliving her experience with Phantom. She wondered why she had been so nervous in the first place. Matthew was so considerate and he made her feel safe and he was so attentive. Now she felt that she understood the appeal of horses, and was anxious to see the relationship between Matthew and his horse.

Besides, she could only imagine how he would look riding Phantom.

He came back in, eyes bright, and grabbed her hand pulling her towards him. "Come on, I have some thing I want to show you before I ride."

He took her to the large barn, walking around to the back. Morning Star and her foal were out in the corral. The foal was running and jumping and stopping fast, and mama was galloping in short spurts, shaking her head, as if she was adjusting her mane to make it look better and acting every bit like the proud parent.

Matthew leaned on the rail with his elbows, his foot resting on the bottom rung of the rail fence. Christina watched, enthralled.

She placed her hand around his waist and he put his arm around her shoulder.

"I never get tired of watching this," he said as he kissed her cheek.

Matthew had been trying to ignore his body's reaction.

He had managed to control himself, more or less since the picnic, but showers were not cutting it lately and he was sure that a ride on Phantom wasn't going to either. It had been too damned long. He cursed his mother and father for their morals and decided that he had to do more than admire her from afar. Car sex came to mind but he dismissed that.

He pulled her head to his mouth and said, "I hate not sleeping with you."

Christina's heart skipped

"Oh, really," she said in a whisper. "I am so done with B.O.B."

Matthew nearly chocked, trying to stifle his laugh. He looked at her. "You are!" his eyes were glowing in the afternoon sun, his chestnut hair glinting. She swallowed hard and he saw the longing in her eyes. He pressed her to him and she felt him hard against her. He kissed her again, only this time she felt the smile on his lips.

He stepped back abruptly and groaned. "I hope this situation is resolved soon. Much as I love my parents, I need to go back home and take you with me."

She said, "Next week the article will be published."

"Good, then there shouldn't be a need for any more of this." In the same breath he said, "Come on, let's go. I need to ride Phantom."

All the while, one of the ranch hands had been observing them, taking special notice of the relationship. The wheels were turning in his head. He smiled to himself as he moved on and returned to the job at hand. A call to Bruno was definitely in order.

Phantom heard them coming and started circling and snorting. As Matthew opened the stall, Phantom was dancing from one foot to the other and shaking his head up and down. Christina was a little afraid of this time. Matthew placed and adjusted the bridle and tied him to the stall. Phantom snorted as Matthew swung the blanket and saddle onto his back.

"What's wrong with him? He was so quiet this morning?"

"Oh nothing, he gets all excited sometimes. He just wants to run."

Looking at the way Phantoms muscles were bunched and rippling with raw power, she wondered how Matthew was ever going to control him.

Leading him outside, she watched with awe as Matthew stepped into the stirrup and swung his leg with practiced ease over Phantom's back, holding him still while he adjusted the cinch, displaying his own ripped muscles under his shirt.

Christina knew that he would look good sitting astride Phantom, but she had no idea just how good. What a handsome pair they made! He was wearing his cowboy hat, and the ever-present gun was strapped to his hip.

Christina almost forgot to get her phone out. She snapped a couple of pictures. Matthew smiled as Phantom circled, getting even more agitated. But Matthew took control, swung Phantom round and they were through the gate and galloping across the pasture before she could draw a breath. She watched them moving in unison, Phantom's tail held high, neck stretched out and Matthew hardly moving above him. This was what Phantom had been so eager to do. He was moving fast and the sun glimmered off his coat.

Matthew could not have been happier. He let Phantom have his head and sat back relaxing as the wind rushed by his face. The distraction was necessary if he had to remain celibate for another week. He wanted Christina in his arms and in his bed every night and knowing she was just the other side of the wall... She was his saviour, he knew that.

Slowing Phantom down, they headed into the trail that led to the river, stopping at the river bank to allow Phantom a drink. After, they crossed the river. He decided to take a different route this time and headed round the bend. Keeping to the riverbank they started toward the other side of his father's property. It was quiet in the woods, except for the birds and a squirrel who did not like the invasion of his territory.

Something caught Matthew's eye ahead, on the rim of the hill, but it was gone almost before it registered. He looked up briefly and decided that it was probably a large bird flying by.

They continued their journey. Phantom, having worked out his anxieties, was walking leisurely along the bank. Matthew was deep in thought when all of a sudden, just as they were passing the cottonwood trees on the opposite bank, Phantom started to become agitated, taking a huge leap sideways, almost unseating Matthew before he took charge. Phantom was not listening to Matthew's commands and jumped into the river. The clatter of hooves and the splashing that occurred caused all kinds of mayhem in the woods. Creatures who had been quite content to allow them to pass uninterrupted just a few seconds before, started up a cacophony. Now Phantom was trying to get as far away as possible from not only the perceived threat the other side of the river, but the noise that seemed to be everywhere. Birds flew out of the woods in front of Phantom's nose and squirrels chattered loudly.

"Jesus, Phantom." Matthew wrestled with Phantom's head, trying to keep him from slipping in the river, or blindly taking off at full tilt.

It took all Matthew's skill and strength to get Phantom back on the river bank. Once there he spoke calmly to him, all the while still trying to hold him back. He was still determined to get away. He shook his head, snorted loudly, and Matthew felt him start to set back on his hind legs, his back end dipping low, ready to take a leap forward. *Here we go.* Phantom took off along the river bank. Matthew held his reins firmly, but knew not to try and stop his progress just yet. If he did, there was a good chance Phantom would just rear up, and Matthew would be dumped in the river. He allowed Phantom to run for a short while, then he really took charge, shortening the reins until Phantom's head was pulled so far back that Matthew could kiss him between the ears or be head-butted if he wasn't careful.

A short distance further on, Phantom seemed to realize that the threat no longer existed and eased his gait just enough.

Matthew pulled him to a stop. They were both panting and sweating by the time Matthew dismounted. Matthew looked him in the eye, and pulling his head down he said, "Whoa, what was that about, fella, you haven't behaved like that for a while. I'm too old to be fighting with you, so let's behave can we?"

Matthew led him to the river and, using his hat, splashed some water on his neck and flanks. It helped to cool them both.

Talking to Bruno was painful, his anger evident as he admonished his cohorts for their inability to find Christina. He had threatened them and they were fully aware of what he was capable of.

Eventually their patience had paid off. For two days they had sat in their black sedan in a hotel parking lot in the next town, keeping their eye on the Mercedes SUV they had followed from Bentley Towers in the early morning hours.

They had their instructions and they dared not disobey. It would be more than their lives were worth.

Now they were holed up in an abandoned cabin in the middle of nowhere, surrounded by fields and cows as well as horses.

"Jesus Christ I hate this, all for that nosey woman. Why can't Bruno just let it go?"

"I don't know, but if that article is published soon... We have to get our act together."

The cabin, abandoned for years, was surrounded by cottonwood trees and whoever had built it had thought things through. The trees served to keep the home cool in the summer and helped protect it from the winter storms. Consequently, it was not seen from above very easily.

They had brought food and water with them and were observing the comings and goings from a distance. The cabin was in a small valley next to a stream and they were able to climb the hill, unobserved, and spy on the ranch through binoculars. Their car was stashed in the lean-to on the side of the cabin. Their light was provided by kerosene lamps, though the windows were covered with cardboard. They were by no means comfortable in there, but they were dry and reasonably well fed except they were not cooking anything. They'd die for a hot coffee.

The situation served to fuel their hatred for Ms. Melville. Why should they be deprived of creature comforts in order to satisfy their boss? He was a mean son of a bitch who only thought of himself.

No expense had been spared to keep her safe. This was born out by the helicopter patrols at least twice a day.

They were thankful for the heavy rain the night they had

arrived, as it kept the helicopter grounded and washed away their tire tracks.

They had formulated their plan. Calderone had contacted them and given them his agenda as well. So at least they had someone who could back them up.

Christina watched Matthew and Phantom until they had disappeared from view. In the distance, the mountains were bathed in the late afternoon sun. Stretching out in front of her, closer to the ranch house, the four rail fences, all neatly painted white highlighted by the sun, framed large pastures in which horses were grazing, their tails swishing away the flies that had started to make an appearance after a cold winter.

The veranda was an idyllic place to sit and contemplate. In front, there were bees, busy collecting pollen from the first flowers. The mosquitoes had yet to make an appearance. It was obvious there was a strong bond between Matthew and Phantom. Christina wanted to share that connection with Matthew. She had felt a connection to Phantom, too, as soon as she had touched him.

A glint caught her eye way off in the distance. She hoped it was Matthew coming back. She waited for some minutes, wishing him to appear. She was being seduced. The city girl had come a long way in a few short days.

She waited in vain. Deciding to be brave, she walked around the side of the barn and leaned on the rail, watching Morning Star and her foal.

The curious foal came over and stood in front of her, putting her head through the fence to investigate. She nudged her knee and blew out her nostrils then started nibbling her jeans. Christina was captivated by the foal. She began to stroke its nose and head.

Unnoticed, Morning Star made her way over. The mare

stood back a bit from the fence. Looking up, Christina saw Morning Star watching her. She reached out her hand as the mare came forward, and now Christina had the two of them up close. She started to speak to them, complimenting Morning Star on her baby.

Matthew had been approaching from the other side of the pasture, pleased with what he saw. Her body language certainly didn't convey anything in the way of apprehension. It made his heart leap. She had no idea.

Morning Star saw him coming and pricked her ears. Christina turned, following the foal's gaze.

He dismounted and came to her. Holding the reins in one hand, he pulled her to him and kissed her cheek. He was sweaty and smelled of Phantom and, underlying that, his own scent.

"What happened to you?" she said, stepping back to better assess his condition. He was in some disarray. His cowboy boots were wet as were his jeans, as far as his knees. His shirt was slightly soiled and covered in splashes of water.

"Phantom got in one of his moods. Something scared him by the river and he took off, very nearly dumped me. Took a bit to get him under control," he said.

While Christina had been concentrating on Matthew, the foal had been vying for Christina's attention, snickering and shaking her head vigorously while standing as close to the fence as possible.

Matthew turned to the foal, amused at the display of jealousy.

"You seem to have made a friend," he said as he stroked the foal through the fence. "You seem to be quite comfortable here, now."

"It just took me a while to pluck up my courage again, that's all. I'm fine now, fearless as ever," she said, putting her hands in her pockets, straightening up and pulling her shoulders back.

Matthew said, "Well then, here" – he handed her the reins. "You can lead him to the barn." She hesitated but he kept his hand held toward her. She looked into Matthew's eyes. How could she resist? She took the reins and with a confidence that belied how she really felt, she said, "OK then. Come on Phantom, let's go." She pulled on the reins and Phantom obliged, turning towards the barn.

Matthew smiled as he followed alongside her. *Welcome back, Christina.*

When they reached the door of Phantom's box, Matthew opened it and if Christina was thinking that Matthew would take over, she was wrong.

"Lead him in," Matthew said.

She didn't really need to as he started to enter on his own.

"Are you coming in?" she said as she started to leave the stall.

"Nope," he said, standing in front of the entrance. "Now's as good a time as any. You might as well take off his bridle and saddle."

She looked at him, a protest on the edge of lips, hesitated and thought better of it. "OK then, I will."

She started by assessing the bridle's numerous straps, and did not really know where to start, hesitating before reaching for the chin strap.

Matthew said, "OK if you don't mind a bit of advice, you need to put his halter on as soon as you remove his bridle; he needs to be secured, that way you can still control him if you need to."

She achieved that with some trepidation but no mishaps.

Handing the bridle to Matthew, she moved to stand in front of the saddle and lifted the flap. She saw the buckles to the girth, and remembered him adjusting them before he took off earlier. She placed the stirrup over the horn and put the saddle flap over her shoulder, in order to gain access to the girth. Pulling the buckles free was difficult, but she managed. Phantom was patient. Grabbing the saddle, front and back, she pulled it off him. It was heavy and slipped from her grip, landing on her foot.

Matthew was there in a flash, picking it up with one hand. "Oh I forgot to warn you how heavy it is."

He looked apologetically at her, and she swatted the top of his head. "Well, thanks, I guess you can't be trusted, good job my foot isn't broken."

On the way out of the box, she thanked Phantom for his patience.

Matthew started to brush him down and refilled his water bucket before leaving him. Christina watched with fascination at the unspoken communication between them.

Once on the way to the tack room, him carrying the saddle slung over one shoulder, her the bridle, he put his arm round her and said, leaning close to her ear, "You did great."

A feeling of satisfaction flowed through her as she kissed his cheek.

Her self-confidence was now fully restored. She was going to embrace this experience, knowing she would grow to love it here, just as much as she loved Matthew and just much as he did.

Surprising her, after putting the tack in its assigned spot, Matthew grabbed Christina, face in both hands and kissed her passionately. He pressed her to him, and she felt the wall, hard and cool on her back and Matthew hard and hot on her front. He continued his kissing, his hot and sticky body clinging to her, his smell enveloping her. She returned his kisses, opening her mouth and letting him slide his tongue over hers, exploring again the sweetness that was there. Her legs were weak now and she almost buckled under him but he held onto her, sighing deeply.

It was not long before he broke away, spinning on the heel of his boot, removing his hat and running his fingers through his hair and walking to the other side of the tack room before turning and facing her.

"Oh God, I'm sorry, I just couldn't resist. Seeing you with that foal and with Phantom, you made me happier than you can imagine."

"Don't be sorry, I was right there with you."

Christina was still leaning on the wall, hands behind her, steadying her. She wanted to go to him, to finish what he had started.

"I have to go now." He hurried out towards the house,. She breathed in, sucking as much air as she could into her lungs in an effort to regain her equilibrium, and then ran after him. Outside, he had turned around, facing her, hands in his hair.

He led her back into the tack room. Her grip tightened as her palm became moist in Matthews hand.

She had no idea what would happen next but she was willing to follow him.

He led her to the bottom of the ladder that led up to the second level of the barn. He grabbed a horse blanket from the rail. "Up you go," he said, looking at the top of the ladder. Without a word she started to climb the ladder. When she reached the top and stepped into the loft, she was pleasantly surprised. It smelled of hay. The sun was beginning to set and was streaming in from the open hatch, highlighting the dust motes floating in the warm air. Matthew came up behind her and spread the blanket on the hay near the open hatch.

His face I was illuminated by the sun, enhancing his sinful good looks as he beckoned her to come over.

He didn't touch her at first. He looked out at the view over the ranch to the mountains silhouetted against the red sky that promised a spectacular sunset.

She followed his gaze and was captive to the sunset as well. They stayed that way until the sun slid behind the summit of the mountain. The barn became dark, as the dusk was the only light that entered the loft. The sounds of the approaching night drifted up to them – activity from the security team, mixed with horses neighing in a faraway pasture. The birds had become silent.

There was a fleeting dark shadow as a flock of bats took flight. The air was still and the sound of a far off train whistle drifted to their ears. They watched the sky become a shimmering jewel and Christina leaned her head on Matthew's shoulder and drew in a breath and smelled the hint of his aftershave mixed with the smell of the hay and horses.

Matthew broke their silence, "I used to come up here a lot when I was younger. I liked the peace that descended at dusk. I would daydream."

She pulled his face to hers and trailed kisses down his cheek to his neck, where the scent of him was the most intense. She inhaled deeply as she undid the first button of his shirt, and then the second one, she moved his collar away from his neck, and kissed him in that spot that sent shivers up his spine. She slid her hand over his chest, delighting in the feel of his chest hair, soft and springy under her palm. He inhaled sharply and drew her to him, kissing her slowly and gently, his lips hot and soft against hers. She slid her tongue slowly across his mouth, parting his lips. Leaning back, taking her with him, she lay by his side, sinking into the soft bed of hay. He rolled over her and buried his head in her shoulder, speaking in a deep husky voice saying, "You are my undoing." His heart pounded against her chest.

He sat up suddenly, running his hands through his hair and down the back of his neck, pausing there, rubbing his neck and closing his eyes.

He took a deep breath. "Come here. Sit in front of me."

Sitting between his spread legs, facing him, she undid the rest of his shirt, pushing it off his shoulders. He pulled her t-shirt over her head and removed her bra. Caressing her breasts, he leaned forward kissing each one, his breath hot over her nipples, fuelling her desire, making her draw in a ragged breath. Undoing the button on her jeans, pulling down the zipper, he pushed her gently backwards and tugged off everything. She knelt in front of him, naked, and did the same to him, carefully removing his holster and his gun. Then she traced her finger down his abdomen following the trail that disappeared beneath his waistband and snapped the button open on his jeans.

They were gloriously naked, the air raising goose bumps and cooling their hot skin.

He pulled her down again and she lay over him, his skin on her skin, touching every inch of his hard muscular body, his heat radiating upwards, keeping her warm on one side, the breeze wafting into the loft keeping her cool on the other side.

Matthew was lost in the feel of her wrapped over him. His heart raced and he ran his hands slowly down her back. He squeezed, pressing her into his arousal.

Absorbing the silky feel of her skin, he stroked the area where her tattoo was. His kisses were soft and passionate as he slid his tongue over her lips, exploring her mouth, lost in the silky warm feeling of her.

Waves of almost unbearable desire coursed through her. She stroked his tanned face, kissed his forehead. Trailing kisses down his neck, feeling his racing pulse, she breathed in deeply, whispering, "Now please, Matthew, now."

He rolled her under him, knelt up between her legs. Anticipation was almost more than she could bear, and she was amazed at his control. Christina watched him as he guided himself to her into her slowly, gasping at the feel of her as she tightened around him. She bit back a scream of overwhelming pleasure as he slowly withdrew and then re-entered her once again, keeping control of himself, guiding himself in and out at just the right speed.

Their lovemaking was slow and passionate and they crested that wave together.

The barn was in darkness by the time they descended the ladder to the tack room floor. They had just started across the yard when someone stepped in front of them, appearing from the shadow of the barn.

Matthew had his gun drawn before Christina even registered what was happening. He shoved her behind him.

It was then that the shadow said in a familiar voice, "Matt, what the hell are you doing coming from there?"

"Jesus, Dan, I nearly shot you. I might ask what you're doing *there*?"

"My job, Matt."

"Oh, well, yeah. I'm sorry, we were, er... how shall I say this, delayed!"

Dan looked at him knowingly and said, "Well, you should let us know what you're up to... That's what the radio's for, remember?"

"Right, I'll remember next time for sure." He took Christina by the elbow and started across the yard. Looking back at Dan he said, "Good job, by the way."

"Thanks, Boss."

They entered the house unnoticed, climbing the stairs quickly. They showered separately, each feeling sated and relaxed.

Chapter 25

Matthew came downstairs the next morning dressed for business: perfectly tailored pinstripe suit, pale lavender shirt and matching silk tie. Christina watched him descend carrying his jacket over one arm and his gun and holster in his hand. His cowboy boots had been replaced with black oxfords. He looked devastatingly handsome, as usual.

"I forgot how sexy you look in your city clothes." She gave him a peck on the cheek as she inhaled deeply.

"Thank you. I have some business I have to take care of today so behave yourself, and let them know your plans, please. I don't want to have to worry about you."

"I promise I will be good."

She watched him walking towards his SUV, and wondered fleetingly why he didn't take the Lexus.

Turning towards the house, she sat in the Adirondack chair on the veranda. She missed him already.

Her attention was drawn towards the corral, where the mare and foal had just been let out of the barn. Christina decided that she needed to get some education on this horse thing, so she went in and retrieved her laptop. She started researching quarter horses and breeding, and how to name a horse.

The time flew by. She had learned a lot, hardly noticing the flurry of activity taking place around her. Leonard was busy talking to Jake about the impending meeting with Mr. Calderone, who was due any time now.

She was interrupted by the sound of a large vehicle approaching down the long driveway, trailing a cloud of dust behind it. It parked in front of the house and a big man in a dark western styled suit got out of the SUV. Leonard appeared from the barn and strode towards him, greeting him with a handshake as he welcomed him to the Double L Ranch. Leonard stepped up on to the veranda and introduced the man to Christina. "Christian, this is our guest, Mr. Calderone."

Christina smiled and said, "Pleased to meet you, Mr. Calderone." She shook his hand. He stared at her momentarily as she returned her attention to the laptop.

She was not sure what Mr. Calderone was here for, but she dismissed it as none of her business.

Dan and one of the ranch hands appeared out of the bunkhouse just as Leonard and his customer were walking towards the large barn. The ranch hand excused himself and diverted to the same barn. As Leonard hurried towards one of the stalls further down, eager to show Mr. Calderone the brood mare he thought would seal the deal, he didn't hear the ranch hand speaking hastily to Mr Calderone, who had hung back.

Christina decided to go to the corral and see the foal again.

The foal came bounding up, greeting her with a shake of its head, which it pushed through the fence towards Christina. She stroked the foal's forehead and greeted her by saying, "Hi, there. I think I have a name for you."

One of the ranch hands came out of the barn carrying a halter, "I'm Bill; you're Christina aren't you? Could you help me get this halter on the foal? She likes you and it might help. She hasn't worn it before and we need to get her used to it."

Christina decided what better way to learn than hands on. "Why not. Just tell me what you want me to do. I don't have any experience, you know."

"Well looks like you're a natural. Even the mom trusts you – see?"

Morning Star was standing off on her own quietly watching what was taking place. "Come inside the corral with me." Christina climbed the rail fence. She moved slowly towards the foal, whose attention was taken with her approach. As she was doing that, Bill was gently touching the foal's neck with the halter. It took only a couple of minutes before he hooked his arm under the foal's neck and over her nose, replacing his hand with the halter, which he slid slowly up her head. The foal only shook her head a couple of times, and then Bill had the halter in place and buckled.

She stroked the foal's head again and Bill started stroking the foal's neck. "This is socializing," he said, "we want to get her used to being touched and around people but we don't want to frighten her. You seem to know instinctively how to connect with this foal. This is your first lesson about horses, right?"

"Yes, I had never even been near a horse before. Don't know why I was so nervous; they are really very thoughtful creatures, and not at all vicious, at least not the ones I've seen here."

"Leonard and Matthew are great with them, although between you and me, I think Matt needs to do some more work with Phantom. He can be a bit of a handful. Some more training would probably rid him of his bad habits." Bill winked at her, and smiling he said, "Don't tell him I said that."

She laughed, "I promise."

Christina was pleased with her lesson, and couldn't wait to see Matthew. She headed back to the house and noticed that Mr. Calderone was still being shown around. He seemed to be getting the grand tour. Passing by on her way back to the house, she caught part of the conversation and could have sworn she heard the name Bruno mentioned.

Still wondering if she had heard correctly, she spotted Liz on her way to the kitchen carrying some glasses.

"Hello, I haven't seen you yet today. How many years and they still haven't learned!"

"Sorry, that's my fault. I should have cleaned up." Christina helped gather the snack bowls and they went to the kitchen.

"I saw you and Matthew coming out of the tack room last night. Did he take you up in the loft? He used to go there a lot. Said he liked the view and the peace at that time of night."

Christina shifted awkwardly.

"Yes, it's quite a view from there and... certainly is peaceful," she said, her face heating with the memory of it all.

"Would you mind telling Len that I have put the coffee in his office, for Mr. Calderone?"

Christina, relieved, retreated hastily and relayed the message.

By mid-afternoon she had learned even more from her research. She was hoping Matthew would return soon. She had chosen a name for the foal and she hoped it suitable.

Just as she was wishing he would appear, her Blackberry rang.

"Hi," she said smiling.

"Hi, yourself, how are you?"

"Waiting for you, I have lots to tell you."

"Ah, that's why I'm calling. I'm afraid I won't be home tonight. I still have some business to take care of, so I will be staying at the penthouse."

"Oh, I was looking forward to seeing your sexy body again."

He laughed, a deep laugh that sent her heart racing. "I like seeing yours too, but unfortunately I will have to dream about it instead."

Chapter 26

By the time the sun was above the horizon she had dressed. She was going to run. It would help get her mind off Matthew.

The yard was deserted and quiet as she headed for the trail behind the barn, diverting for a minute to go into the barn and see the foal. There she was, in the stall with Morning Star. The foal greeted her with a whinny and Morning Star came over, putting her head over the door. Christina petted her and said, "Your baby is beautiful. I have a name for her, Morning Star. I think she should be called Venus."

As she was leaning in to the stall she felt something land softly on her head. She realized that it was hay. She looked up, staring into the blackness. Dismissing the incident she headed out of the barn by the back door, and jogged to the trail to begin her run. The sun was up now and it promised to be a beautiful sunny and warm day. She felt herself starting to get into the rhythm and just kept running. The air was just right for a good workout.

She found herself at the edge of the pasture before she knew it. There was a small trail that led into the woods and she decided to follow it. She was in no hurry to return. Something in her head told her that she should have stopped at the edge of the woods, remembering what Matthew had said. *Shit.*

It was obviously the trail that Matthew took Phantom through on his way to the river. Curiosity guided her. She had all the time in the world and waiting for Matthew to come back was driving her crazy.

She jogged along the trail, listening to the sounds of the woods, squirrels chattering their warning to stay away, birds chirping in the trees. She suspected something bigger than a squirrel was scuffling through the under growth but these sounds were unfamiliar to her and she was not really alarmed.

Slowing to a walk, her thoughts turned to her situation. She was delighting in the new experience of family dynamics, but wanted to remain strong and independent. Feeling independent again she was ready to take charge. Perhaps this was why she hadn't thought to tell anyone where she was going.

Hearing the distant flow of a river, she walked on and arrived at a clearing in the woods, stopping along the banks. She sat on a rock and listened to the river. It was soothing. She let it wash over her.

As she sat there, there was scrabbling in the underbrush behind her. Just as she turned, a large man leapt forward and grabbed her with both hands.

Her Grav Maga training kicked in and she managed to sweep him off his feet with one move. He landed hard, knocking the wind out of him. She started to run but another man appeared. He was fast and he caught her by the arm, holding her long enough for the first man to regain his footing. She struggled and kicked at them but soon realized she was no match for two men.

While the larger of the two held her arms down, the other tied her wrists together behind her back. They gagged her and without a word started to drag her along the river bank.

When they reached a bend, Christina saw where they were going. They kept going until they were opposite the cabin. It was situated behind some trees and could have easily been missed at first glance. There was a fallen tree spanning the river at that point and they directed her across it. Having a hard time maintaining her balance with her hands tied behind her back, and the fact that she was now scared to death, she almost lost her footing a couple of times but she was steadied by the bigger man.

Her mind was working overtime. She knew Matthew was not going to magically appear and save her a second time. So, she was on her own. She tried to remember Matthew's lecture, about staying safe in enemy territory. She breathed deep and forced herself to stay calm as they led her into the cabin.

When she entered, they pushed her towards the bed and forced her to sit. She complied, not wanting to make them mad.

When her eyes adjusted to the dimness, she saw that the cabin was mostly empty. The windows were covered with cardboard. She had no idea who they were or what they wanted. Were there more of them than these two? Perhaps they were escapees from a jail somewhere. They had been living like this for a while, as they were scruffy and didn't smell too clean.

There were lots of empty boxes and food wrappers on the floor, along with plastic drink bottles and some crushed beer cans, leading her to the conclusion that perhaps there were more men somewhere else. The bed she was sitting on only had a sleeping bag and a grungy pillow. The couch was definitely the worse for wear. It was sagging and dirty, and worn out in all the usual places. There didn't seem to be a bathroom.

All of a sudden she had a frightening thought. After all, if they had been on the run for a while, they might be looking for a diversion. Up until this nasty thought had entered her head, she had been quite calm really, hoping that she could figure a way out of this. Now she was shaking with fear. No one had spoken a word yet. She sat still, watching them.

The big guy pulled a cell phone out and made a call.

This was the first time that anyone had spoken and when she recognized the voice, her mouth went dry. It took a great effort not to react to his voice. Why hadn't she recognized him?

How stupid! She was here supposedly safe with all the protection Matthew could supply. She berated herself for her false sense of security. Now what was going to happen? The last threat had been bad enough.

She heard him say, "We've got her, what do you want us to do now?"

He listened for a minute.

"OK we'll try."

After he replaced his phone in his pocket, he approached her menacingly. She held his stare. She was not going to be intimidated by him again.

He leant over her. Removing her gag, he looked into her face, only inches from his. She smelled his rank breath and his body odour and turned her head to one side. He pulled her face back to him. "You," he spat out, "don't listen very well, do you? I am not kidding when I say we are all fed up with this assignment. Look at us, we don't like living like this.

"I suppose that fancy boyfriend of yours thought he could fool us. Well guess what? Here we are. Now, you have been told what to do so make it happen. Call whoever needs to be called and kill the article. If you don't... You know how this could end, right?"

He shoved her back onto the mattress.

She lay there for a minute catching her breath, then she tried to sit up.

Once she had struggled into a sitting position, she asked, "What do you think I can do now?"

"Well I want your phone, for a start."

He undid her hands and tied one hand to the bed.

He started searching her, running his hands over body; she breathed in deeply and resisted the urge to spit at him and slap his hand away. Instead she shrugged her shoulders away from him and turned her head as he continued sliding his hands over her. She could not endure it any longer so she grabbed his wrist hard stared unblinking into his eyes as he made to slap her face and said resignedly, "It's in my back pocket." He shouted, "If you know what's good for you. NOW!"

She fished her phone from her pocket, found Jack's number and gave it to him. He pulled out his burner phone and, stepping outside, dialed.

Christina didn't hear what was said to Jack.

She was anxious to find out what their demands were but

she wasn't about to ask.

On his return he crushed her phone under his foot.

Chapter 27

Matthew was busy all day catching up. His office however was humming along even in his and Dan's absence.

Anne was her usual efficient self and had kept everything ticking along. Her cheeks were glowing when he greeted her. She smiled.

"Mr. Bryson, so nice to see you. Your mail is on your desk. Coffee today?"

"Thanks, Anne. Yes, coffee would be good."

He set to work and cleared his desk, staying late in order to do that. He left after everyone else but still had time for supper before his late night meeting. It was about a forty-five minute drive to get there so he was in no hurry.

He sent a short text to Christina saying he hoped she had a good day, he would miss her tonight.

Leaving Leo's after supper, went on to his meeting and when he left he was confident that it would all work out for him. He slid behind the wheel and, not looking forward to it, started to head back to his penthouse. He was cruising along, his music playing, when he started thinking of Vivienne and his heart ached again. He hadn't thought of her for a while.

He slept fitfully and woke early wasting no time getting back to the ranch. Once there he went directly across the yard to the small barn. He fed the horses and brushed Phantom, all the while talking to the horse. Phantom was an excellent listener, no answering back, only a few grunts and snuffles of agreement as he promised him a ride later in the day. Matthew then cleaned the stall and found the hard work soothing.

He was unsettled for some reason, a condition that he had not experienced for quite some time. Being here usually had the opposite effect. He went to the tack room. On his way to checking his equipment he looked up at the ladder and smiled. When he finished cleaning his saddle it was breakfast time.

Matthew dropped his boots by the bench. He was assailed by the aroma of breakfast as his mother attended the stove. She turned, surprised to see him as he came up behind her and kissed her on the cheek; he greeted her with, "Good morning, Mum, are you ever going to get away from this stove?"

"I doubt it. What are you doing here so early?" she laughed lightly.

Matthew looked around, "Oh I didn't want to leave in the rush hour traffic. Have you seen Christina this morning?"

"Not yet."

Surprised, he asked, "Was she tired last night?"

"I don't know, Matthew. I was upstairs most of the evening working on my quilt. I think she stayed in her room."

She usually arrived at the breakfast table long before this. Perhaps she was not feeling well. He left the kitchen and went to the front stairs. He looked up to see if her door was open, then climbed the stairs two at a time and knocked. His heart began to pump as he knocked again, this time louder and more rapidly. Perhaps she was in the shower? He waited a second or two, listening.

He burst through her door taking in her room in one fell swoop, his hand already on his gun. He reached the bathroom in three long strides and flung open the door, knowing the answer before he entered.

He ran out and leapt down the stairs as he had gone up them, rushing out the front door, hailing Dan on the radio as he ran full speed across to the bunk house, entering just as Dan was heading for the door.

"Where the hell is she Dan? Where the hell is she?" The

colour had drained from his face.

Dan gripped both of Matthew's arms and said in a calm voice, "It's OK, Matt, we'll find her. She can't be that far."

"What do mean she can't be that far?" he shouted. He ran his hands through his hair and he started pacing the floor as the rest of the team were assembling in the common area. They all looked shocked and stared at their distraught boss.

Matthew yelled, "This can't be happening again."

Dan began to organize a search of the property.

Once he had that in hand he addressed Matthew, "When did you talk to her last, Matt?"

Matthew stood by the table, holding himself steady with a white knuckle grip on to the back of one of the chairs. He stared at Dan in desperation.

Dan tried to calm him. "I know, Matt, it won't happen again. I swear we will not let it. We won't let it. I will die first."

Matthew drew a deep breath. He felt like he could at least think now. His adrenalin was still pumping but he had come down some. He thought for a minute. "I saw her yesterday morning before I went to the office. I told her to tell you what she was up to. Did she?" He looked hard at Dan.

"No."

"I texted her last evening, after my business meeting."

"OK. Well, we can try tracing her cellphone. I'll get someone on that now. In the meantime, you and I can take the helicopter up. We haven't done a sweep today."

Everyone was engaged in their tasks. The search of all the buildings and wooded areas in the immediate vicinity yielded nothing.

Both Matthew and Dan headed for the helicopter, driving there in silence. It was only a short distance but it seemed like a long way. They were in operation mode now so there were things to plan and things to achieve in a short period of time.

Once in the helicopter, everything became automatic for them, they went through the pre-flight check in record time and were soon airborne.

They started gaining altitude. "OK, they abducted her, so what now?" Dan was asking the question.

"I don't know, Dan. I don't know. I do know they can be violent. They have already killed her informant and he was an undercover cop."

"Do you know who her editor is? When will it be on the shelves? I expect they have made a demand to someone, or...." Dan paused.

Matthew's head flew round and he stared at Dan, horrified.

"I hate to voice that scenario Matt, but we must face it."

Matthew was silent, and paled at the statement. He felt sick now and nearly threw up. Swallowing hard, he took a few deep breaths as he looked Dan in the eye. "THAT cannot happen. We have to end this nightmare so let's not dwell on failure."

Just as he finished his sentence there was a sound and a small hole appeared in the window beside Matthew; he ducked automatically as he felt the rush of air whizz past his cheek and the bullet bury itself in the bodywork beside Dan's head.

"Shit shit shit," yelled Dan.

He immediately pulled the helicopter up as fast as he could to a safer altitude.

"OK. We need to figure out where she is. Christ, Dan! What the hell. Guns. I never thought they were that desperate! Do you see anything down there? Fuck, fuck... too many trees here."

Dan was concentrating on flying and didn't answer.

Matthew, breathing hard, pulled his gun but it was useless at this altitude and there was no way he could see where the shot had originated.

They calmed down and concentrated on the landscape below, flying over the ranch methodically. There were no signs.

Nothing looked as if a vehicle had passed recently. There was the abandoned building but no tracks led in or out. Nothing looked as if there was any recent activity. The only thing different was the fallen tree over the river. Matthew dismissed it as having happened during the storm, a few days ago. They continued their sweep and returned to the landing spot.

Once back in the bunkhouse/command center, Matthew learned they couldn't trace her cell phone.

He relayed their experience and yelled at all of them for not keeping her safe.

They maintained their silence avoiding his stare and keeping their heads down trying not to cringe as he admonished them and slammed a chair against the wall as his final act of frustration.

He had reviewed the logs from the day before and the previous night. Nothing seemed unusual and they had performed their patrols as per instructions.

He needed to talk to her editor.

He made the call. Jack said he was relieved that he had called told Matthew a demand was made just a short time ago. They wanted the article stopped or she would be killed.

"When is it due on shelves?" he asked.

Jack replied, "Next week, Tuesday." He sounded desperate. "Thank God you called. I am beside myself here. I was just looking for someone to call, apart from the police. You run that security company don't you?"

"Yes I do," he said, hardly able to maintain his composure.

"How do you know they have her?"

"I asked that question as well. They told me she had a small butterfly tattoo on her shoulder. Does she? I don't know but I had to assume she did." Matthew's heart stopped. *Jesus.*

He told Jack he was going to find her. He sounded far

more confident than he felt.

Jack said he could not stop the publication now, even if he wanted to.

He reassured Jack that he was on the case, asking Jack not to call the police; he would contact AJ if he had to. God, he hoped that would never happen.

Returning to the main room he tried to piece things together. No one had seen her since the night before. He had texted her. They traced her cellphone and she had used it in the vicinity of the ranch.

She had been with his parents in the evening for supper and drinks. Then, she had gone to her bedroom.

Eventually he sat down and no one dared interrupt him.

Suddenly he jumped up and ran outside to find Dan.

"She likes to run, she likes to do that early in the morning. Surely, though, she would have told someone what she was up to."

"OK. Let's see what we can find on the trail."

They walked the trail, guns drawn but didn't see anything that led them to think she had been abducted there.

They went back up the trail disappointed.

Matthew was becoming more and more despondent.

He returned to the bunkhouse and reviewed the daily reports again. Nothing unusual there that he could determine. The night patrols had been done, too. He came to the one conclusion that had some merit: she had gone running.

He ran back to the house and searched her room, he didn't see her running shoes but started opening and closing drawers quickly and searching the closet. She had definitely gone running.

So they returned to the trail and started looking again. Reaching the edge of the woods, near the trail he had taken Phantom down, Dan discovered footprints covering some of Phantom's hoof prints. Matthew was elated. For the first time since this nightmare started there was hope.

They checked their guns and took off into the woods. It was logical to assume that she had stuck to the trail, so they were able to follow her tracks all the way to the river. Once they got to the rock she had sat on, they only had to look around to see that the ground was disturbed by more than her foot prints. There were large footprints in the dirt, as well as a flattened area in the grass. They determined there were two people, as well as Christina.

Matthew was all for carrying on down the river bank, but Dan discouraged him. "We have to go back and come up with a plan for the rescue operation. It's still the middle of the day. We don't even know if she is in the vicinity or if they took her elsewhere."

Once inside the bunkhouse he asked for reconnaissance reports of any activity by the river. No activity was reported. Matthew stopped for a minute and tried to remember what he had seen when he was out with Phantom. He had certainly been a bit preoccupied with Phantom that day, but something bubbled in his memory, yes, there had been some kind of building, on the opposite side of the river. He then recalled the tree they had seen across the river.

Intuitively, he knew it had not been blown down by the storm.

"Dan, I'm going to take Phantom out to the river and follow the trail as far as it goes to take a closer look at that abandoned shack. It'll be less suspicious than the helicopter. Phantom took a hissy fit there, last time I rode him. I didn't think about it then but we must've been observed. I'll radio if I need help but I will just take a ride, see what I can find out."

Dan was not in favour and strongly tried to discourage Matthew. "Matt stop being an idiot. You... we, are not prepared and you are the first one to tell us that preparation is the key to success."

Matthew yelled. "Well what the hell do you want me to do Dan, sit here and wait for a shot to ring out?! I'll be damned if I will do that again."

He flung the door open and headed for the barn.

Once there, he began readying Phantom. "OK boy, here's the ride I promised you."

They took off at a gallop following the track and then trotted into the woodland trail. He slowed at the tree stump and assessed the ground. He was right – they had headed towards the abandoned shack.

Anxiously following the river until he was close but still hidden, he crossed without incident. They moved down the other side of the riverbank, Matthew drawing his gun as he approached the shack. He checked that his wireless com unit was working, relaying information to the bunkhouse.

He watched Phantom's ears intently.

Inside the shack, Christina was still tied to the bed. Her abductors were seated at the table, severely pissed off at their situation, their guns set in front of them.

She could not hear what they were whispering but hoped they were waiting for instructions before they simply decided to shoot her and leave.

Suddenly a shadowed passed over the cardboard-covered the window. Her eyes widened. Her mind raced. Was it her rescuer? Was it part of the gang who abducted her?

As she was trying to decide her next move, the decision was made for her. One of the men said he had to go outside. He left the table, scraping his chair on the floor in his haste to exit the shack.

Phantom reacted to the noise and Matthew immediately pulled him to a halt. He was behind the shack. He started stroking Phantom's neck, hoping it would keep him quiet. The door creaked open. Matthew took the safety off, still unsure of how many there were. He waited.

He had no evidence that Christina was there or even alive but he had to go on the assumption that she was both. Staying where he was, he listened for the door again. The river was drowning out a lot of the noise as it flowed past the shack. He heard someone call out, "Hey, Joe. Go get some more water from the trunk will you?"

He heard the door creak once more and stayed still for another few seconds. Then he turned Phantom back toward home.

When Matthew returned to the ranch he immediately sought out Dan. They spent the next few hours strategizing and then their plan was ready. Two of their men set out on foot do some observation with night goggles and a parabolic microphone. An hour later they came back and reported that without a doubt there were definitely more than two, Best of all, they'd heard Christina ask for water.

So, she was alive. He was so relieved it was hard to maintain his demeanor. Leaving he stepped outside and moved to the side of the small barn. Taken by surprise he slid down the wall and cried with relief.

They planned a rescue in the early morning hours.

Hours later, two men took the suburban and found the dirt track that led to the shack. Guarding the only exit, they would wait until being told to proceed once she was released.

Four men, including Dan and Matthew, hiked back in. They crossed the river and stationed themselves one on each side of the shack. Listening with the parabolic microphone they determined that perhaps one of the captors was asleep.

Matthew insisted that he and Dan be the ones to enter the shack. He knew it was a case of déjà vu, but he needed to lay the demons to rest, and this was the only way it would happen. There was no option for failure.

Once he and Dan were prepared, his heart slowed and he was calm and focused on the task ahead. After convincing himself that this was not as difficult as trying to rescue Vivienne, he indicated to Dan that they were to commence.

Back down the track the men in the suburban were sitting, their guns locked and loaded and sitting on their laps. Talking quietly, they didn't notice the movement beside the truck until it was almost too late.

Mid conversation the doors were ripped open. The reaction was fast and one perpetrator was dead from close range, shot between the eyes.

The second one on the driver's side knew he was going to die next. Lucky for him the driver was impeded somewhat, by the steering wheel and took a few seconds longer. The guy dropped his weapon and took off into the woods pursued by both men. He was out of shape and no match for the men from Midnight. When he was caught he pleaded for his life. They obliged and simply told him to run. He did in the direction away from the shack.

Matthew and Dan worked very well together. They heard the shot and reacted fast. Access was gained with a battering ram. The door flew open on the first hit, flying off its rusty hinges. Dan threw in a flash bang.

Their enhanced night vision found one guy on the floor, holding his hands over his eyes. The second guy had his gun pointing at the door. Matthew dropped him with one shot.

Dan reached the other guy in a couple of hurried steps, and placed the gun to his head, daring him to move. He didn't. A movement in one corner alerted Matthew. He aimed and fired, the body hit the floor and the gun skittered toward Dan.

Matthew took in the rest of the room and immediately saw Christina tied to the bed a gun against her head. She was terrified, blinded by the flash. The gag slipped from her mouth as she screamed and started to struggle against the restraints on her wrists.

He flew across the room, pulling his goggles down to hang round his neck and shouting, "Christina, Christina, it's me, you're OK." In the midst of the gun fight taking place inside and out, he reached for her, grabbing her upper arm. She resisted his hold and tried to pull away until realization soon overtook her and she didn't say anything, she just cried. He made short work of the rope around her wrists and then he had her in his arms, sweeping her off the bed. In one smooth move he fell to the floor dragging her with him to keep her out of the line of fire as guns blazed in the darkness and the sound of bullets filled the air. He lay on top of her and joined the gun fight. She scrambled out from under him and rolled under the bed. Covering her ears, she lay face down praying.

It felt like an hour before the shooting finally stopped. The air was full of cordite and she was still lying with her ears covered when Matthew peered under the bed with a flashlight. He touched her arm and she jumped, pulling her self further under the bed. She opened her eyes and saw his. He helped her out and picked her up, carrying her out of the shack as he stepped deftly over the dead bodies in his haste to get her out. She clung to him with a fierce grip around his neck.

The chaos that had reigned was short lived. Against the sounds of his team securing the area, all he could hear now was his own heavy breathing and Christina's sharp panting breaths gushing over his face. He removed his gun, helmet and night goggles.

Christina finally calmed enough to accept that she was safe. She inhaled him as she felt his strong arms encircling her. She began to relax her grip on his neck and then she was kissing him desperately. He returned the kisses and then pulled back and looked into her eyes.

It was dark, but a shaft of moonlight played on her face. She was alright, and he started to believe that it was all going to turn out fine now.

Chapter 28

Matthew had decided that he would go directly to his apartment with Christina. It was only an hour away, and he did not want to bring chaos to his parents' home in the middle of the night. He had charged Dan with the cleanup and the explanation to his mother and father. He would go back there tomorrow with Christina. In the meantime, he needed to have her to himself.

She had fallen asleep in his arms in the back of the sub-urban. He was still wearing his gear but he was content to keep her there until they arrived at Bentley Towers.

"Wake up angel, we're here."

"Where are we?" she said, sleep still clinging to her.

"At my place." He helped her out of the vehicle and walked her through the front door, leaving his gun behind in the safe keeping of his men. The night security guard was surprised to see them and stared curiously at Matthew, still dressed as he was in combat gear and escorting a very dishevelled woman. His eyes widened, but he refrained from comment. "Good mor-ning, Mr. Bryson."

Matthew acknowledged his greeting with a nod and con-tinued to the elevator.

Christina, now fully awake, smiled at him as they entered the elevator. She continued to held on to him tightly.

When they entered the apartment she relaxed. Matthew felt it as he released his hold on her.

He placed his keys on the rack.

As she settled in to the couch, leaning her head back and closing her eyes she said, "I was really wondering if I would see this place again."

Matthew removed his bulletproof vest and combat boots, dropping them where he stood. "Remember, I promised I would always have your back. I keep my promises." She looked down at her clothes and was shocked at the state of them. She pulled her t-shirt off.

"Oh Matthew, I owe you again!"

"You do not owe me anything. I am the one indebted to you. How about I run the bath for you?" he turned and smiled at her again, a smile that said it all as he walked into the bathroom taking her t-shirt with him and dropping it in the hamper.

Following him she watched as he tested the temperature, wondering how she had been so lucky to find him. He was strong and kind. He had killed for her. That was a sobering fact. She was not reticent anymore, she really wasn't. She needed him. She loved him. She knew now that he would not disappear.

He turned. Rising to his full height he approached her, touched her face with his warm wet hand and said, "Here let me help you." He started removing her clothes gently and unhurriedly. He felt something so indescribable when he touched her. His heart swelled with love. Yes, he had to admit that it was love after all.

Christina felt the change in him as he helped her into the bath. She sank into the warm jasmine-scented water and smiled inwardly as she inhaled deeply.

She looked at him and said, "Please, join me."

"Are you sure? I don't want to do anything that might upset you after your experience."

"You will upset me more if you say no."

"In that case..."

He settled behind her in the large copper tub. She leant back, nestled between his legs, as his arms encircled her torso. He kissed her neck and whispered in her ear, "I am so happy right now." He took some of the bath gel in his hands and started smoothing it over her shoulders and back, smothering her tattoo with his hand. It felt so soothing.

Her heart started to race and her breathing quickened.

Her breasts swelled under his gentle strokes. He washed her hair and rinsed it under the hand-held shower. She had never experienced such caring and love before, no one had ever caressed her with such gentleness. No one had ever expressed their love to her like this. No one had ever loved her like Matthew did. She melted into his caresses, absorbing every touch. Every movement of is hands on her body soothed her and released every bit of doubt she ever had about him.

She felt content not acting on her desire right now, staying in the tub until the water cooled.

Matthew made the first move. He kissed the top of her head, bringing her out of her euphoric state. "Come on, we need to get out of here."

She turned to him and kissed him on the mouth. "Thank you. You do know how much I love you don't you?"

His smile cast a spell over her.

He stood first and the water glistened and ran down his perfect body, splashing her as he helped her to stand. Her eyes never left his and she watched them darken. He grabbed a towel from the rail and began to dry her hair.

When he was done she took another towel from the rack. He stood still, absorbing her touch as she slid the soft warm towel slowly over him, drying the droplets that slid seductively over every plane and edge of muscle. She paid special attention to his forearms, delighting in their hardness and sheer size. She knelt in front of him as she continued her journey down his body.

Standing in front of her, watching as she adored his body, his desire evident, stealing his every breath with her touch, he could not resist anymore. He bent down and gently lifted her to her feet. He picked her up, carrying her to his bed, setting her on her back at the edge of the bed. He knelt in front of her and kissed her stomach as he caressed her breasts, rubbing his thumbs over the hard peaks of her nipples and tasting her desire. She opened up to him, unable to resist his warm soft breath as her core tightened and her orgasm began to build and roll up her body. She arched into his mouth and could not control her movements any more, fisting her hands in his curls and massaging his scalp. She felt his hands trembling around her waist as she shattered like crystal. He enveloped her as he climbed on top. Her heart was filled with love as he found his own release, shuddering and losing his breath as his orgasm overtook him.

Feeling sated, lying face to face, held in Matthew's loving embrace, in Matthew's bed, basking in the afterglow of the most exquisite sexual experience of her life, she inhaled deeply. She traced her finger over his brow, ran it down the length of his nose, then placed a kiss over his hot soft lips. She caressed his cheek while her fingers took hold of his slightly mussed-up curls above his ear. Her hand moved slowly down the side of his face, to his neck where she felt his wildly beating pulse. He absorbed her touch, relaxing beneath her palm as she continued her slow progress delighting in the feel of his silky skin, then her hand travelled to his shoulder where she felt every sharp angle of his muscles, and her journey continued as she caressed him all the way down his rib cage, fingers rippling over him past his waist and up to the crest of his hip bone, sliding down his thigh and following the length of the scar, the only imperfection on all of his six-foot-three frame, sliding her palm around to his smooth hard buttock, moving her hand up to the small of his back and gently pressing his body into hers, so that there was not an inch of him that did not make contact with her.

After her terrifying experience she had never felt so safe. It was as if nothing in the world would ever hurt her again. Matthew placed his leg over her thigh and she melted into his body. This was where she needed to be.

Matthew's intense lovemaking had been exquisite.

He had buried his head in her neck and whispered, in a husky sensual voice, at the height of his orgasm, "I love you

Christina." She had felt his hot tears running down her neck and her own tears mingling with his.

Lying thus, Matthew began to talk. Holding her even tighter, he said, looking up to the ceiling, "I don't know if I could have survived losing you as well. My life was so empty after Vivienne.

"I was so focused to do it right this time. Both Dan and I were as determined as we have ever been, trying not to make the same mistakes."

Christina lay there hardly breathing for fear she would interrupt him. She had been waiting for this since finding out about Vivienne's death. She remembered the times she had tried to get him to explain. He had shut down. This was a night of firsts.

She had given herself to him wholly, knowing that he could not do the same. He had told her so, but she was prepared to wait. She knew it might never happen, but had lived in hope.

She saw the deep sadness reflected in his beautiful eyes. She felt his body become tense, his jaw tighten.

"Go on," she whispered to him, "it will be alright, I am right here."

Matthew shifted uncomfortably, took a deep breath and said, "I don't think I can relive that again. I thought I was tough enough to withstand anything that life threw at me. I have been in dangerous situations. I think I am brave. Neither of us thought for one minute that we would fail. We had never failed before. Vivienne's life depended on us. We did our research carefully, or so we thought." Matthew paused, the recognition of some detail passing over his face. His eyes were glistening.

Christina wanted to stop him right there, but she reasoned that if she didn't encourage him to continue, there would be a part of him lost to her forever. "Please continue, Matthew, I know it is the most painful thing that you have ever done but you need to forgive yourself."

"I don't think I can ever do that. She was my whole world. I thought about her constantly. When I was deployed, I would find love notes tucked into some piece of my equipment or pocket. It was the thought of her that kept me going, during hard assignments, that drove me to make sure I would return, as I always promised her I would.

"Vivienne had volunteered to help deliver food in Somalia. The first thing I heard – on the news – was that three aid workers had been taken hostage and their interpreter and driver had been shot. I had not heard from her that day. I wasn't overly concerned, sometimes it was hard to get messages out. I saw a picture of the three workers. Tied up and sitting on the dirt, in a small hut. Terrified. I looked closer, and there was Vivienne. She was battered, had a black eye, part of her shirt was torn off..." Matthew brushed his tears away vigorously with both hands.

"She had put up one hell of a fight but was was hit with a rifle butt to the head. I remember hearing someone yell 'No' and realized that it was me. I jumped out of my chair and almost collapsed on the floor. The room was spinning. How could this be? Not Vivienne. I started pacing in circles gasping for air. My phone was buzzing insistently. It was Dan. He told me stay put, said he was coming.

"The first thing he did was pour us both a large scotch.

"When my sanity returned, our training kicked in and we knew we could get the resources together. We didn't know how long we had, didn't know their demands. They wanted the world to know that they had done this. That was all we knew. Dan and I worked on it all night, then he went home.

"I tried to sleep but that proved fruitless. All I could see was Vivienne's terrified face. By the next morning everyone in our firm had heard the news. It was buzzing with conversation. Then everyone fell silent..."

Matthew's crying had stopped. He paused and looked at Christian. "Do you want me to stop? It can't be easy for you hearing me talk about her like this."

"Matthew, let it out, free yourself. I would like to know the rest. Go on please."

He shifted position and said, "This is the hard part. "Dan and I arrived in Somalia a week later. We thought six of us should be enough. No one knew we were coming, except the organization she volunteered for. At least that's what we thought. We had plenty of firepower and were prepared for anything. The director of the aid agency told us they had not heard any demands. We knew where they were being held. We spent that night holed up in a ditch. God that was uncomfortable.

"We could see the camp layout, figured out what hut she and the others were in. We had the attack all planned out by dawn. It was hot as hell.

"When night came we launched our attack. There were eight of them. They were taking turns, four on, four off, patrolling the perimeter. We knew where their leader was, a different hut. We heard them talking, arguing, maybe over ransom. There seemed to be dissension, short tempers. Not good at all. We knew we didn't have much time.

"We attacked from two sides, killing all four of the guards. You don't need to know how," he said, looking directly at Christina. "It was quick and silent.

"We made it to the hut. Dan and I slipped inside. We whispered to the hostages to keep quiet, we were going to get them out there. We realized there were only two..."

Matthew's voice cracked, but he continued.

"Where was Vivienne? The leader's hut, they said. This changed everything. We freed the two we'd found, had to carry them outside, passed them off to our comrades and headed in a dead run to the other hut. We hoped to take them by surprise, burst through the flimsy door, guns at the ready..."

At this point, Matthew leapt out of the bed. He strode to the wall both fists clenched and placed his hands flat against it and rocked backwards and forwards. His head bowed between his arms. Every muscle on his back flexed constantly.

He continued to talk to the wall, almost in a whisper. "She was there, gagged and tied to his bed, naked, her head moving wildly from side to side."

He slumped against the wall as if he would fall to the floor any second. Christina resisted the urge to go to him, to gather this broken man in her arms.

"The leader had his pistol aimed at her." Matthew's voice rose, almost to a shout, "I hesitated for two, two fucking seconds. Oh my god, Christina," he yelled, "before I could get a shot off, he shot her."

Matthew almost fell, but steadied himself against the wall.

"Dan opened fire and that, that monster, dropped to the floor... I was screaming Vivienne's name, but I knew she was dead."

He paused and turned towards Christina, agony etched on his face. There was a long pause and then more quietly he repeated, "Two seconds, that's all."

Shaking, he stumbled back to the bed, and collapsed on top of her sobbing uncontrollably.

Her sobbing joined his and in an effort to calm him, she started caressing his back, soothing him. After a while they both lay there holding each other, as if their lives depended on that one embrace. Their tears abated and with arms wrapped around each other, finally they fell asleep.

Chapter 29

Christina woke first. She lay still, listening to Matthew breathing evenly beside her. He looked serene, and she never tired of admiring his fine features, his face flushed with sleep and his hair mussed up. His arm lay across his chest and she admired the contours of his biceps and his forearm.

He had admitted that he loved her. She hoped he had forgiven himself for not saving Vivienne. He would always have Vivienne in his heart, she knew that, but it was part of what made Matthew, Matthew. She hoped she had been responsible in some small way for putting him back together.

Matthew woke unusually late for him. He lay alone in bed. Where was Christina? Panic gripped him, but only until the smell of the coffee drifted to him.

He stared at the ceiling, reflecting on his admission, he felt free, giddy with the revelation that at last he could move on, never forget, but put his failure in perspective. Looking at the empty space on his dresser he said a silent goodbye to Vivienne.

Now where was Christina? He left his bed, pulled on a pair of sweatpants and went looking for her.

There she was, wearing his iPod, her hair in a ponytail, swaying as she danced around the kitchen preparing the coffee and looking for breakfast, or by now maybe brunch. She had her back to him, and once again he had the good fortune of seeing her very shapely rear end. She had borrowed one of his shirts and she had tied it in front, around her waist. Were those his boxers she was wearing?

He leaned on the counter watching her, admiring her, smiling as he followed her movements, as she jigged around unaware of his presence. Yes. He had made the right choice. He knew now that she was the only one who could have rescued him from his despair. It had been a year of darkness and now he was ready to live again. She was going to be a handful, what with her independent streak and her bravado. Well, he welcomed the challenge.

He rounded the counter and grabbed her by the waist with one hand, swinging her round in a circle, lifting her off her feet. Leaning on the counter he set her down between his legs pressing her to him, amusement dancing in his eyes, his suspicion confirmed.

With a look of surprise on her face, she smiled widely and removed the ear buds. He kissed her on the mouth, chastely, saying between kisses, "I. LOVE. YOU."

She kissed his nose and then his lips. "I love you, too."

He picked her up, turning effortlessly, placing her on the counter. Standing in between her legs, he stroked her cheek "Do they fit OK?" She smiled and nodded. "You are amazing you know. Last night was amazing. Thank you for listening and for understanding. His expression changed slightly, his brow creasing, "When I woke, just for a second I wondered if maybe you had left."

"Why would I leave?" she answered.

He kissed her again, slipping his hand inside her shirt, placing it over her breast, He pushed the shirt aside, and he slid his hand round to her back, exposing her breast to his gaze. He breathed deeply as he fluttered his tongue over her nipple.

Her heart started its staccato rhythm and her skin heated. Her abdomen rippled with pleasure. She placed her hands flat on his chest, feeling his silky skin stretched tight over his tanned muscles. She stroked her hand down his arm, from biceps to wrist, feeling the hardness and the blush of fine hair. Matthew suckled on her nipple and her breasts swelled. His other hand began a slow smooth caress down her back as he pulled her closer to him. Reaching down he wrapped her leg round his waist and picked her up, still kissing her breast as he carried her to the bedroom.

"I need you right now, I need to be in you right now," he said as he gently placed her on the bed, kissing her forehead.

"Turn on your stomach," he said.

She obliged. He climbed on the bed beside her and began kissing her shoulder, where her tattoo was. He traced its outline with his finger following it with a kiss. Moving her hair away from her neck he kissed her nape, sending shivers down her spine. Her fists clenched and unclenched the sheets, as his caresses set her on fire. She began arching her body off the bed in an effort to make contact.

"Shhsh, shhsh, angel, soon enough. Let me love you, Christina, wholly and completely. My heart is full, my body aches for you. I need to taste you. Trust me, let me love you."

Restraining her with one hand, he trailed his tongue down her spine, interspersing it with kisses. He caressed her back slowly, his fingers feather soft as they slid over her creamy skin. The fire was lit in her now, and she was groaning deep in her throat. She didn't think she could wait any longer for him, but he continued his caressing and then she felt her orgasm begin to gather and start to roll upward deep inside her body. He parted her legs and passed his thumb delicately over her sex. Pleasure rolled through her body, sweat bloomed over her as she sucked in deep breaths.

He continued his journey, kissing the back of her leg, paying special attention to the back of her knee, making her wriggle under his hand. He kept up the journey, reaching her ankle and then her toes. She was breathing so hard now she was sure she would faint. Stars exploded behind her eyes, her fists clenched and unclenched with greater speed now.

All of a sudden she was on her back, looking into his eyes.

He entered her, sliding slowly into her heat. He withdrew and slowly re-entered her. That was it. Christina could not contain herself any longer, she cried out his name and buried her face in his neck, wrapping her legs around his waist allowing him deeper penetration. He followed with his own prolonged release, whispering "I love you" as he did so.

They collapsed in a heap gasping, and then he was beside her, kissing her face. They both trembled as he held her firmly in his arms.

They stayed that way for a long time. Eventually, their breathing slowed and their heart rates returned to a more even rhythm.

As thought returned, she turned to him and kissed his chest, following it with a soft gentle touch that made him shiver. "Will it always be like this?" She smiled up at his flushed face. "Because if it is I will need some serious work outs just to keep up."

He laughed out loud, and she loved the sound.

His good intentions of returning to the ranch first thing were now in jeopardy. They remained in bed until it was mid-afternoon.

All of a sudden they heard a key in the door. Matthew was the first to react. He jumped out of bed and closed his door.

Christina whispered "Who...?"

"Gracia," Matthew whispered back. He ran around searching for his sweatpants, hastily putting them on.

Christina could not help laughing at him. Matthew was grinning as well, aware of his behaviour. "Stop laughing at me. I have put her through enough lately. Be kind."

Gracia was not alarmed this time as Matthew appeared in the living area. Besides his equipment abandoned on the floor, she had noted the aroma of coffee.

"Mr. Bryson, you *are* here. It's been a few days now. How are you? More to the point; how is that lovely girl?"

"Yes, Gracia, I'm back, at least for now. Christina is fine, thanks. In fact, she's here as well."

Gracia looked towards the bedroom. She had a small grin on her face, and a twinkle in her eye, as she said, "Sleeping late, is she?"

"Gracia! What are you implying?" his eyes challenging her.

"Nothing, Mr. Bryson." She held his gaze. He shifted his stance and changed the subject.

"Now that you are here, do you think you could prepare us something to eat please? It's been a busy time and we arrived late."

"Of course, an omelet and some salad perhaps?"

"Perfect. I'll let Christina know; we will be back in a few minutes."

It made Gracia happy that he had someone in his life now.

She looked around the living room sighing she began straightening up his apartment. It really was in disarray.

Chapter 29

"You are staring at me."

"Oh! I'm sorry, I was admiring you again, and I was just thinking how much I loved you."

Not taking his eyes off the road, he smirked and said, "A lot I hope."

"So much that it hurts."

Leaning towards Christina, his eyes still on the road, his voice hitched, he said, "You know that I've loved you ever since we met, don't you? I just couldn't admit it until I thought that I might lose you. I couldn't let go of Vivienne either."

Kissing his cheek, she whispered, "I know."

Touching the top of his thigh, running her hand down his leg, she felt his muscles tense as he shifted his back against the seat, inhaling deeply.

She watched as his mouth twitched up to small grin and his eyes widened. He was happy, and she vowed to keep him that way.

"I hope everything is OK at the ranch," she said, a hint of anxiety etched in her voice. "They won't be angry, will they?"

She entwined her fingers with his. Matthew, watching the road, looking ahead, said, "We'll be there soon enough. Your article hasn't be been published yet and we still have security there. I feel bad about bringing so much chaos to the ranch."

"From what I have seen, your parents love you, they believe in you. I wish I had even one parent, who could have given me what your parents have given you."

He squeezed her hand, bringing it to his mouth and kissing the back of it. "You are fine just the way you are. Beautiful, strong and fearless and, you did it all on your own."

Driving down the road to the Double L ranch, she gripped his hand even more firmly.

The ranch ahead was bathed in the evening light. It looked welcoming, a place of comfort and security.

Chapter 30

Matthew was finally happy and excited at the prospect of showing Christina how life could be. He was going to do all the things he had longed to do with Vivienne. He was not going to wait. He was not going to waste a second.

He would begin today.

Sitting in the ranch house with his parents and Christiana, he placed his arm around her shoulder, inhaled the jasmine scent that lingered in her curly hair, and whispered, "Let's go and see Venus. She'll be glad to see you."

Christina smiled at him, stroking his thigh, making those sparks ripple up his leg and beyond.

They rose from the couch. Matthew looked at his parents and saw their amused and pleased faces. He winked at his father.

He took Christina's hand, leading her toward the mud room, resisting the temptation to kiss her on the way there but once out of view he pressed her against the mud room wall and kissed her passionately. She responded in kind and they were both breathless.

They put on their boots and headed to the corral.

Watching them approach, the sun shimmering off her coat, Venus's ears pricked. As soon as she recognized them, she came skipping over to the fence, whinnied a greeting and proceeded to nudge her head through the rail.

Christina was amazed and delighted, "Oh Venus! I missed you too."

Matthew was even more delighted

That's my girl.

Matthew watched as Christina kept talking to Venus. He didn't say anything, just watched. In his heart he knew they were a pair.

"Come, let's go see Mum's horse. She's in the other pasture. I can see her over by the cottonwoods."

Christina was enraptured by the whole experience.

She spent the rest of the day familiarizing herself with Jasmine, a beautiful Appaloosa with a chestnut body and white-spotted rump and two white socks on her hind legs.

Matthew left her to it and went back to his father's office, where he found

Leonard at his desk speaking on the phone, negotiating with Mr. Calderone, discussing when the mare would be ready to breed. He silently acknowledged his father's presence and proceeded to call Ty who was still in the Sudan. Things were going well and the unrest seemed to have abated. He hoped that he would be able to bring Ty home soon. He deserved a rest.

After hanging up, he checked his calendar. Christina's article would be on the shelves in just a matter of days. And then it would all be over, right?

Staring out the window the failing light, he watched Christina and realized that the last pieces of the puzzle that was his life had finally, finally been put in place.

R. Ann Steel was born in England and emigrated to Canada in 1970. Married with three children and four grandchildren, she loves horses, horseback riding and reading. Her love of romance novels – the escape from the world, the happy endings – led her to try her hand at writing one. That result is *Matthew & Christina: A Love Story*, and now a sequel and other romances are in the works.

R. Ann Steel resides in Saint John, New Brunswick.

65687985R00148

Made in the USA
Charleston, SC
31 December 2016